KNOT YOUR BASIC B*TCH

HIGH FRUCTOSE CORN SYRUP VERSE

MIYO HUNTER

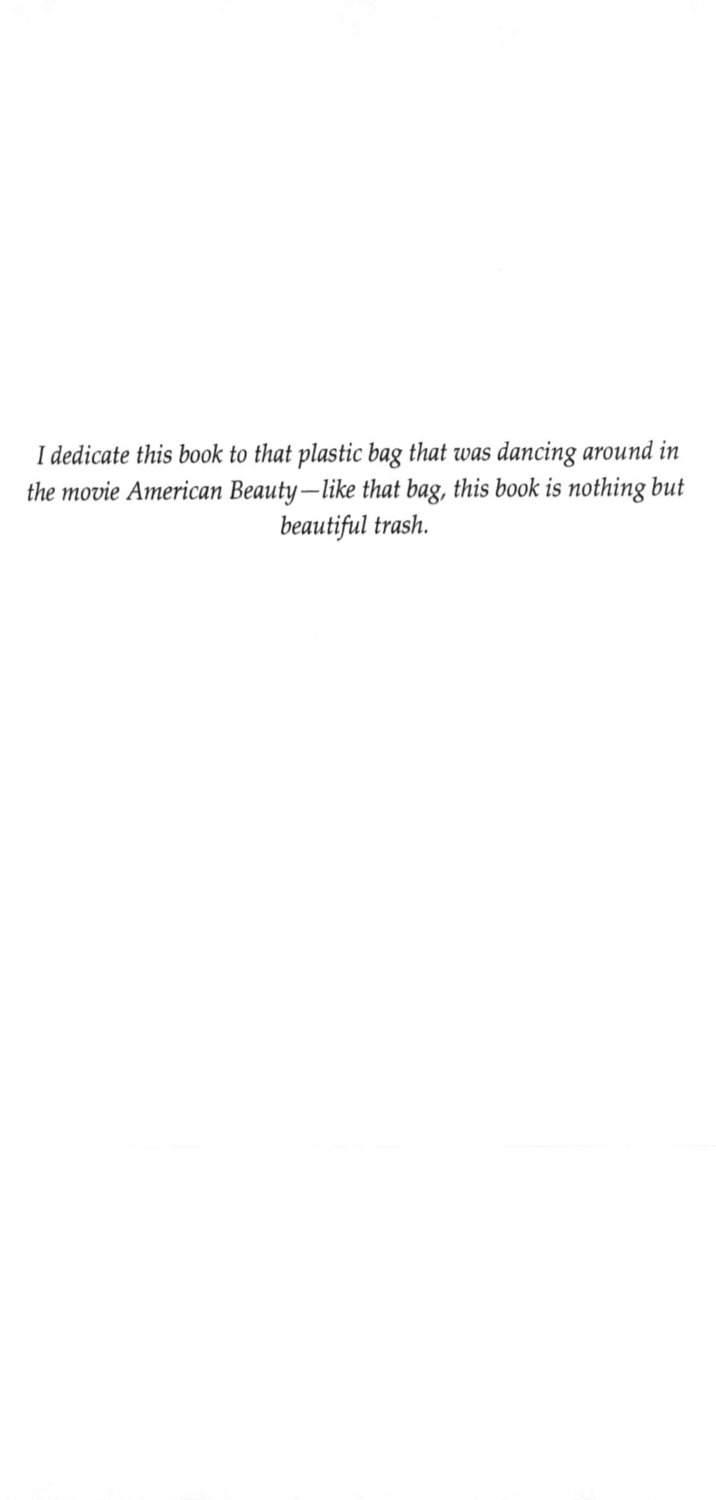

I dedicate this book to that plastic bag that was dancing around in the movie American Beauty—like that bag, this book is nothing but beautiful trash.

CONTENT WARNING

This book contains cursing and mature sexual situations. If you object to that, this is not the book for you.

Part of the story includes a trip to the aquarium. The sum total of my research for this scene was drunk googling and watching *Finding Dory.* This is the High-Fructose-Corn-Syrup Verse not the National Geographic.

THE STRYKER PACK

Moms (2):
Rain, Momma Rain
Estelle, Mother

Dads (6):
Diesel, Papa Diesel
Genesis, Daddy-Gee
Ragnar (pack lead), Father
Locust, Daddy-Lo
Magnum, Mag-dad
Phoenix, Pa Nix

The kids in age order:

Sisters (8):
Rebel (omega)
Avril
Cashmere (omega)
Chloe (omega)
Bronze
Blue

Aphrodite
Rose

Brothers (8):
    Ember (alpha)
    Gunnar (alpha)
    Titus (alpha)
    Zane (alpha)
    Cash (alpha)
    Rowan
    the twins—Hunter and Logan

[Both moms are pregnant again]

CHAPTER 1
CHLOE

GOD, all I wanted was just a little bit of peace and quiet.

Rose, my youngest sister, was screaming at the top of her lungs because Zane had taken the last of her favorite yogurt.

Zane was holding both hands up like he was warding off a storm, "There's two cups of strawberry and three blueberry in—"

He was cut off by more screams like she was being murdered. I don't know why Zane was trying to reason with a three and a half year old, anyway.

Just one. One quiet morning. That was all that I was asking for.

I sighed, abandoning the last of my cereal, tipping the rest in the trash. It was just too loud. Two of my brothers and one of my moms had popped into the kitchen to see what was happening.

I was halfway out of the room as she started screaming again. Pointing her chubby fingers at Zane. "He took it! He promised he wouldn't, and he took it!"

There didn't seem to be much hope of this not turning into an even bigger thing.

It really didn't seem to me like a huge ask. Just a little bit of quiet. A little bit of space. But growing up in a pack with two moms and six dads made that completely impossible.

Why was having a quiet morning so hard? It's all I was asking for. This day shouldn't be so crazy already. It was only eight in the morning.

Back in my room, I reached for my noise canceling headphones, but it wasn't on my desk. Or knocked on to the floor. I doubted it would be under my bed, but a quick look confirmed it.

Who touched my stuff? This time?

"Cash, do you know where my headphones are?"

"Laundry room!" He yelled in my general direction.

The groan I made could only be described as the enraged battle cry of a wild hippo.

Cash took them sometimes to listen to music. Just grabbed them off my desk when he wanted to go workout.

If he just used them, and then put them back where he found them, that would be fine. But *no*. Too many times he'd forget. Dumping them in a pile of his sweaty gym clothes.

So maybe I was counting down the days until I was off to college and old enough to go out into the world. Get a room that I don't have to share.

In my secret dreams, there was nothing better than being able to just sit in a quiet room. Maybe with a cup of peppermint tea, and a good book. Plenty of betas got to have quiet office jobs. I could be something like a secretary, for some calm job. Like the front person at a small dentists' office. Or maybe a librarian.

Something perfectly boring.

I was destined to be a beta. It was fine. When I was little, maybe I'd had a brief moment of delusion when I thought I'd want to be an omega like my moms. Have my own pack that was devoted to me. How they would help me with everything and worship the ground that I walked on. It all sounded great in theory.

A devoted pack of men was less appealing when you grew up with eight brothers. Had to hear all of them belching and watch the awkward middle school years when they still thought it was okay to pick their noses if they thought that they could get away with it.

Six packs weren't so impressive, when it seemed like all my brothers managed to have one. And most of my brothers seemed to be allergic to shirts. Just running around, flaunting chiseled bodies like a bunch of cavemen. Even Gunnar, and he didn't even go to the gym. Just sat around hogging the TV and eating all the donuts before anyone else even got a single one. How were genetics even fair?

No matter what age they were, *all* of them managed to leave their socks everywhere.

I swear to God, there isn't a single room in this deodorant-forsaken house that doesn't have at least one smelly teenage sock lying dirty and crumpled in the corner somewhere.

There was no way in hell I wanted to deal with having my own pack.

Maybe my parents were all on to something when they'd given me a beta name.

I wanted to have a cool name. The Steamy Aura's Weekly always had lists of the most fabulous omega names.

My brothers and sisters all had cool names... But by the time it got to me, all my parents just started to run out of creative steam.

It was like my other siblings had names taken straight out of the top most interesting names for up and coming alphas and omegas. Zane, Titus, Gunnar, Cash, Rebel, Avril, Bronze, Blue, Cashmere and Ember.

Then they got to me.

By then, they'd just collectively scraped the bottom of the barrel to think of something.

My name is Chloe.

Can you get any more basic and boring than that?

I have a sister who is literally named Rebel… How is it that my moms and dads could look at one of their infant babies and think that she was a badass Rebel. Then look at me and go.

Oh. Hmmm. That one looks like a Chloe!

The thought made something twist in my stomach.

If it wasn't so noisy, I'd be able to eat the rest of my cereal and I wouldn't feel hungry right now.

It made me so mad I was starting to feel hot. I shook my head angrily as I rummaged through piles of unfolded laundry, looking to find where my headphones could be.

Did someone knock over a bottle of perfume in here? Or laundry detergent? With all the noise, and the fighting downstairs, and the heat, this flower smell was the—

"Is somebody perfuming?" I heard someone scream from downstairs.

Oh great. More chaos.

I mean, that wasn't fair. I'm sure that all my sisters were going to be thrilled.

Which sister was it this time? Blue was a little young. Was it Bronze? But she was at soccer practice…

Besides, the smell was coming from nearby.

I heard a rumble of footsteps and jostling, before the door to the laundry room slammed open and Gunnar, Titus, Zane, and Avril were falling over each other.

They all turned to stare at me.

"What?" I snapped at them.

None of them answered. Titus had an expression that was downright sheepish, as he rubbed the back of his head. Gunnar was staring at one of the laundry baskets like it contained juicy secrets rather than sweatpants.

Zane was my only sibling who cleared his throat to say, "we were trying to figure out who perfumed."

"Yeah… and?"

I stared back at them expectantly, but they were all staring at me like I had grown a second head.

If they wanted to go find who was perfuming then why were they standing here staring at...

Oh.

Oh, *no*.

No, there was no way.

I was perfuming?!

That meant... that I wouldn't ever get to have my quiet beta life. I was an omega. Most omegas grew up dreaming about their pack.

Yes, it sounded ideal. It was everyone's dream... everyone's but mine.

...As more of my brothers and sisters piled into the room, I could just picture it. My own pack of men who would do anything to keep me safe.

And in the process, leave their dirty socks everywhere.

Great. Just great.

CHAPTER 2
CHLOE

I THREW my stress ball into the air, catching it before it smacked me in the face. Only to launch it as close to my ceiling as I could again.

"You need to take this seriously." Zane was pacing with his arms crossed. He was going to wear a path into the rug if he kept this up.

"I don't understand why I have to go to the Institute. I don't even want to learn anything about alphas." I refused to look at stupid Zane and his stupid pacing. Besides, if I took my eyes from the ball, it was going to hit me in the face.

"Don't let our moms hear you say that. Especially not Mother. I saw her puking in the kitchen."

"Oh, come on. Don't tell me that she's pregnant again. Mother said that she was done after Rose. Momma Rain's already like five weeks?"

"Six and a half. And Mother can't help it. She has a breeding kink."

"Ugh, come on. I didn't need to know that. I especially don't want to know how you know that."

"Anyways, forget about that. What's your grand plan if

you don't want to go to the Institute? You can't be saying that you want to go gold-pack."

"What's so wrong with ending up as a gold-pack?" I threw the ball harder so that it whacked against the ceiling, before hurtling back down.

"Besides the fact that you could legally end up dark bonded? The fact that you wouldn't be able to have any kids?"

The no kids thing wasn't the end of the world. Not that I hated kids or anything. Or put any thought into wanting them myself or not. I'm just saying, that watching my moms puking and waddling around everywhere... making comments about how they felt like walruses... watching them struggle to get in and out of a car for God's sake—let me just say that it didn't exactly make me thrilled by the idea of getting knocked up.

But getting dark bonded was another story. It was essentially legal slavery. Alphas, who would have complete control over me.

There's no way that I could allow that to happen to me.

No quiet secretary job was worth that.

"Fine, I can go to the Institute, and get the stupid shot. But can't I just come back after that? Do I have to stay there?"

"What were you planning to do instead?"

"I was planning on applying to New Oxford University. My grades are good—"

But Zane was already shaking his head no. "They don't let omegas just skip the Institute to go to college."

"There's no law that says I can't apply." It's true. I looked it up and everything.

"Well, our parents would probably let you apply if it's what you really wanted. But, Chloe... you'd still have to take all the Institute classes."

I caught the ball in my hand, then opened my palm fully

so that it rolled away from me. Bouncing off to the floor below.

I sighed deeply.

None of this was fair.

I don't know who I had to blame. Should I blame biology, when I was an omega and some other girl who was desperate for it would never be? When I wanted to be an omega about the same amount as I wanted to lick pond scum.

Should I blame society? And the way that it just shoved omegas into the same category.

Until it felt like I had no other choice. I was placed neatly into my box, simply because of my designation.

Why should I have to take classes at the Institute when I'd been a straight A and B student? What sort of information did they decide that omegas need to learn? Why should I put off *my* college classes? Who decided that it was necessary for me to learn about alpha and omega biology?

It made me want to grit my teeth, and prove them all wrong. All of them.

"Fine. I'll go to the Institute."

CHAPTER 3
CHLOE

I HAD OPENED up to an entire chapter that was literally titled "Testical Play."

How the fuck was I supposed to take myself seriously, while reading about the nerve endings on a ball sack? This so-called 'textbook,' came complete with diagrams that I'm sure did their best to make testicles not look like wonky meat sacks.

It's not like I don't find men attractive—I do. But that didn't mean that I wanted to read an entire fifty pages on balls—the different angles to stroke, the rhythms, rolling them, tapping them. Who knew they were so complicated?

Why did balls need all of this attention?

I don't know. Maybe if they were attached to someone I cared for, I would be more motivated to learn about the benefits of manual versus oral stimulation, and various kinds of lube. But right now, none of this information was all that appealing.

Luckily, the ball research was the only homework assigned for tonight. It gave me plenty of time for my *real* learning.

My moms had relented and helped me sign up for an

online college. All it would take was a few online classes each semester. I should be able to finish my online degree at the same time that I graduated from the Institute.

I cracked open a book and got to work.

Though the Institute hosted far more omegas than it did alphas, there were still entire facilities dedicated to alpha bonds—both the clinical and social aspects necessary for forming them. There were designated sections for alphas to meet, and decide which members they wanted to include in their packs. The alphas had event calendars and meeting areas for them to work out bond formation. The Institute also had all the medical clinics and registration offices that alphas needed to make their packs official.

Though it was never meant to be an area for alphas and omegas to intermingle, there were some areas where it just happened. The cafeteria tables were a major unofficial meet-up spot.

I texted Titus which table I was sitting at. I'd picked a spot outside of the cafeteria, near one of the willow trees. There were clear blue skies, and relatively comfortable picnic benches. There was a nice breeze, and it was far less crowded out here.

Titus was a bit older than me and had been busy with training, so I hadn't gotten much time to hang out with him recently. He was at the Institute to start sorting out forming a pack of his own. Being here might be absolute crap, but I was looking forward to hanging out with one sibling, rather than a freaking dozen or more at a time.

I'd loaded a tray with a caesar salad and an apple turkey sandwich that looked pretty good. The food in the cafeteria wasn't bad, but it came with the potential luxury of getting to eat it at a table that wasn't already over-crowded with six or ten of your siblings. Especially when it was one of my brothers who got to lunch late and would then ask me mid-bite if I was planning on finishing whatever it was that I was eating. Utter lunacy, eating with siblings.

I dug my textbook out of my bag, opening it to the reading for the day. I'd probably be able to knock off half of my homework before Titus got here. Even though staring at my sandwich, I could already tell which side had the most perfect bite. It was tempting to start without him, especially since Titus might ask to 'try' some of my food, and end up taking a monster bite out of it. But we *had* agreed to meet for lunch.

I'd just gotten into the flow of reading when a shadow fell across my picnic table. I frowned at my sandwich. Titus said he wouldn't get here for another fifteen minutes. So who…

"What's a pretty little redhead like you doing out here all by your lonesome?" I looked up to see a bro-ey looking guy. I could just tell by the look on his face that his idea of the pinnacle of an intellectual conversation was about the exact content of his protein shake, and the optimal time to drink it in order to get the most gains. By his orange cream scent, I could tell that he was an alpha.

The alpha had a wide smile on his face like he'd said something incredibly charming.

If only he'd said something charming… something at least interesting enough to make it worth losing my train of thought as I was working on my studies.

I smiled wanly back, hoping for the right combination of polite and disinterested.

"Homework."

"Learning about alphas? I could give you a hands-on lesson. Help you learn *exactly* how to please a man."

Was there a polite way to tell a guy that he was a giant cheeseball and I was suddenly lactose intolerant?

I had more important things to learn than how to please a

man. Is that the only thing people thought I was going to learn here?

Shit... Was it the only thing I was going to learn here?

"I'm fine. I grew up with loads of brothers, and they all seem to be growing up into alphas. I'm good." Okay that came out a little more incest-y than I meant it. But I could literally ask any one of my brothers or dads anything, and they'd help me... or beat up any of my problems if I ever needed it.

"For some weird reason, I don't believe you." He had that stupid smile on his face again.

What?

Did he think that I was lying... about having brothers? Why the hell would someone lie about that? I didn't dignify his statement with a response. Instead I stared at him blankly, hoping that he would take the hint and just go away.

He did not go.

"Tell me your name, darling."

"Why should I tell you my name? I don't know you."

The alpha frowned. Like my words suddenly pierced through the fog of his delusion enough for him to realize that I actually wasn't interested in him. A thought that didn't quite register with him, as he smiled again, as if he took my reluctance as some kind of challenge. Like I was playing hard to get.

I was not playing hard to get. I did not want to get gotten. Why did no one seem to understand that?

He leaned in closer and lowered his voice as if he was telling me a secret. "I for one, am the top pick for the new Stryker pack. So you should stick with me. Can you picture being the omega for the Stryker pack? Who wouldn't want that?"

Eww.

The Stryker pack? As in Titus Stryker's new pack?

Who wouldn't want to be the omega for Titus's pack?

Well his sister for starters.

Hints were not working for this guy. It was time to get more direct.

"No, I'm not interested."

The guy gave me a look like I was crazy.

"Look, you must not know who the Stryker pack is. Their parents were absolute legends. The dads in that pack took down four terrorist plots that would have de-stabilized the government and caused massive civilian casualties."

"Five. But who's counting," I muttered. Not that the guy noticed. He kept going like I hadn't said a word.

"Their moms were absolute beauty queens. They were Valedictorian omegas at the Institute, and made the top of the lists in all of the omega magazines. Either one of them could have been celebrities if they'd wanted to."

I shifted in my seat a little. It was kinda weird to know that a guy had a hard-on for your moms. I was so used to thinking of them as the givers of band-aids and the kissers of boo-boos. The readers of bedtime stories. Not the stuff of this stranger's wet dreams.

"Now their kids are growing into alphas and a bunch of their daughters became omegas. Word on the street is that every single kid in that family is drop dead gorgeous." He had a smirk on his mouth, as if this guy was giving me privileged insider information, instead of just telling me awkward stuff I didn't need to know about my own family. "I was too young to make the cut for Ember Stryker's pack. That was formed a few years before my time."

I vaguely remember Ember complaining at the dinner table about some kid-alpha who'd kept nagging him for a chance to join his pack. Could this be the same guy? What would be the best way to ask?

"But now Titus Stryker is looking to make a pack of his own, and I had a highly promising interview with him last Tuesday."

"Uh huh," I said because he was looking at me expectantly, waiting for me to say something.

"So what do you say? A gorgeous thing like you should be with the best. Stick with me, and I'll make sure that you become the omega of an elite pack."

Behind my unwanted admirer, Titus was walking up to our table with an overloaded lunch tray, hesitating as if he was worried that he was interrupting something. I waved him over.

Saved by the brother.

As soon as he saw my brother, the guy's entire voice and posture changed. When the dude looked into my brother's eyes, I swear to all the gods that he blushed all the way to his ears. Not in a—oh, you caught me being disrespectful to your sister—way. More like a DAMN you're fine, kind of way.

I cocked my head at my brother, to try to see what it was that this bag-of-dicks saw in him.

Purely theoretically, I recognized that my brother was an attractive guy, I guess. Like I'm not blind. I can see that his features are all proportional and what-not. He has that square jaw and rugged physique that could be on the cover of any steamy magazine cover. Then again, it was also a biological fact that it was physically impossible to rate a guy's attractiveness when you watched him grow up in the awkward phase before he discovered how to use deodorant correctly.

"Hey, Titus! Were you looking for me?" He was practically batting his eye-lashes at my brother.

Titus gave me a side-eye, as if to ask me, why does this guy think I would be looking for him?

The alpha raised his hand like he was warding off an attack. "I'm sorry, I had no idea that this was your omega."

"His omega?" I echoed.

What did he think that I was? A possession? The most delicious and prized cut of the steak. Or some fancy car or something.

"Uhh…" Titus scratched the back of his head, like he knew that he was missing something. "Dorian, this is my sister."

Dorian turned his face slowly away from Titus to look back at me, and his face went pale. I could imagine him thinking over every word he'd just told me, as the cogs in that thick noggin of his figured out what he'd done.

I gave him a little half-wave as if I was meeting him for the first time. Might as well have been. Figures this guy needed to listen to another man to get introduced to me properly. He'd just tried to mansplain my own family to me.

"It was a good thing you talked with her anyway," Titus was giving me a calculating look that I did not trust at all.

I narrowed my eyes at him, trying to silently communicate with him that whatever nonsense he had up his sleeve that he better knock it off. *Now.*

Titus smirked, as he kept going.

"Chloe is going to help me interview the alphas who want to be a part of my pack."

No.

Nope. Not a chance.

I had too much on my plate already. That was *not* something I would…

"I'm glad that we were able to have our little chat then." Dorian grinned at me, like he and I were in on a little secret together. Like our conversation had gone phenomenally well and all his little Stryker dreams about coming in my brother were about to come true.

Had he even heard himself talk? Did he honestly think that I had a decent impression after all of that?

But before I could correct him, and let him know that my brother was severely misinformed about my willingness to help his stupid cause, Dorian waved as he walked away from our table.

Just a few feet away Dorian was already on his phone,

probably texting all the other alphas on campus how well his "interview" went with me. After news like that got out, there was no taking it back.

If what Dorian was saying was true, all the alphas were chomping at the bit to get into Titus's pack.

I'd done my part to keep a low profile. Not answering all of the questions I knew in class. Not bringing up my background. And just like that, with one short conversation with my brother, and a few text messages, my quiet life at the Institute was irrevocably ruined.

CHAPTER 4
CHLOE

"I'M GOING TO KILL YOU." I glared at Titus.

"Nah, you love me."

"You did not just tell him that. People are going to get the wrong idea. Like they are going to have to get *my* approval to get into your stupid pack."

"No. That's why it's a brilliant idea. I trust your judgment."

I rage bit into my sandwich. Right into that perfect spot. It was still tasty, but it would have been better if everything didn't look and taste like the little pocket of peace I'd managed to build for myself here was all about to come crumbling down into the dust.

I sighed and dropped my sandwich back onto my plate.

"That guy was absolutely wet for you."

"A lot of them are like that." Titus frowned, like dealing with his own hotness was a real problem for him.

I rolled my eyes.

"I don't want to help you form your pack." I thrust my plastic fork into my salad, though my poor lunch did nothing to deserve my wrath. Angrily swirling the romaine leaves around in the caesar dressing.

"Well, that's why you are perfect for it. Since you don't actually care about my pack, the guys will really have to stand out for you to say something nice about any of them."

"But that means I am going to be drowning in all the alphas who want to get into your pack. Do you think that I want that?" I took a bite, angry that it was delicious.

Great, now I was mad at my salad.

"I can't believe that you're complaining about me getting you loads of attention from guys."

"I can't believe that you're doing this to me." I muttered.

"Come on, Chloe. Give me your honest feedback on the guys. No one is better at calling out bullshit than you are. You wouldn't want me to end up with a pack full of assholes?"

I chewed my salad thoughtfully. Did I trust Titus's judgment in picking his own pack?

Obviously not.

If Dorian was being honest and that was an example of Titus's top choice, then yes my brother was in for a world of problems. Titus would probably make a pack with a literal psychopath, torturing omegas and making everyone generally miserable. Or stuff his pack full of the hottest guys who somehow all had the absolute worst emotional baggage.

"Fine," I huffed.

"You're the best."

"And you're the worst."

CHAPTER 5
CHLOE

THE NEXT DAY everything went normally. I turned in my short essay on the nutritional content of semen, and studied for a quiz that I'd have to take on Friday. None of the other omegas treated me any differently, like they heard the news that I was a member of a mildly famous pack. I shoved my textbooks into my bag and breathed a sigh of relief. So far, so good.

I headed past neat rows of desks, frowning when I heard a chorus of giggling up ahead. That didn't sound like the—haha your joke was very funny—laugh. No. It was the—Oh Em Gee, there is a really hot alpha in close proximity, is he looking?—kind of laugh.

As soon as I stepped out the door…

Ugh, what was it now?

"Hey!" An alpha who I'd never met before, with all the bouncing and infectious energy of a golden retriever, was smiling at me like I'd just told him the winning lottery numbers. "You're Chloe Stryker?"

Fuck. He did not have to say that so loud.

Most of the girls had already left the class, so maybe I

could… No. Nope. That curly haired brunette was whispering to the other girl. I'd forgotten her name, but I *did* remember that she was some kind of gossip magnet. Seriously, she had all the best tea. Basically, the drama coming out of her mouth was the only thing distracting enough to get me out of study mode. Which was great. Except that now, it seemed like I was going to be the subject of it.

"Yeah… you're here because of that thing for my brother?" I was trying to keep it cool. Downplay it enough to bore gossip girl's attention and hopefully get through this day with my anonymity intact.

"Yeah! Your brother Titus said that anyone who wants to get into his elite pack needs to go through an interview with his sister, Chloe. That's you right? Daughter of *the* Stryker pack? Like the ones with the dads who literally stopped terrorists and everything?"

With every word, I found it harder and harder not to press my hand against the alpha's mouth to force him to shut up.

I could practically feel the brunette's eyes bulging at the news. She looked torn between writing it all down, and running off to tell everyone the good news. Instead, she paused, pulling out her phone, typing away furiously.

Double Fuck.

"Yup. Okay, let's get on with it." I turned and marched down the hall towards the nearest entrance. Just stopping short of dragging this alpha after me. As if getting out of here ASAP would do anything to mitigate the damage already caused.

I mean, my brother had already sort of ripped the floodgates wide open. I was just kinda hoping that I'd have a day or so more before they utterly drowned me.

I didn't stop until I was sitting at my favorite table, and pulling out a notebook. If I was going to suffer from the embarrassment and the publicity that my brother was putting me through, I would at least do a good job. Who knows? Maybe with my help, my brother would actually end up with a decent pack after all.

"Alright then. What's your name?"

"I'm Noah Reid."

I nodded, jotting it down. Then I paused, drumming my fingers against the table. I never did figure out exactly how I was going to do this. Honestly, I'd hoped that I'd have a little more time before all the men started coming after me.

I figured that I'd just ask them some simple questions and see if the men ended up merrily swimming in a sea of red flags.

So far, I wasn't getting any weird vibes from this guy. Nothing creepy or sociopathic yet. At the very least I was in a public space in the sunlight, so I probably wasn't going to be murdered or anything like that.

Honestly, Noah the alpha seemed perfectly nice, and only a little bit stupid.

I leaned back at the table, getting comfortable.

"So tell me, why do you want to join my brother's pack?"

———

It was only the first day of Titus's ridiculous plan, and already I was stuck interviewing three alphas. It was starting to cut into my study time.

How was I going to prove my academic potential if I didn't ace my quiz on the erogenous zones around the anus and within the anal valves?

What about the geometry homework that I had with my online classes? What if this little project pushed back my time-line to graduating?

It was fine. This was fine. I could handle it. I would just have to shuffle things around.

Skimming over my notes, I decided what exactly I would include in my text to Titus.

Me: Interviewed Jagger. Nothing technically wrong with him, besides being fucking annoying.

Titus: Really? You thought he was annoying?

Me: The guy wouldn't stop talking about what he found hot & not, and THEN started giving me suggestions.

Titus: You think he's going to piss off other omegas?

Me: He's attractive sure, but I'd rather eat glass than hook up with him.

Titus: What about Blade? What did you think of him?

Me: Blade is the first guy I've spoken to who wasn't trying to get into your pants.

Titus: Really? He wasn't into me?

Me: I think he's just straight

Titus: You think he'd be good for my pack?

Me: Well, he's not a psychopath. So he's got that going for him.

Titus: That's high praise, coming from you.

Me: If you want me to say nice things about the guys I'm interviewing, pick better guys.

I hit send just before realizing that what I'd texted was probably the worst thing I could have told my brother if I ever wanted to be free of all these stupidly attractive men.

CHAPTER 6
CHLOE

MY DAY WENT NORMALLY—UNTIL lunch.

The cafeteria had salmon and asparagus, which was great because it meant that I was meeting my goal of being healthy. Obviously as a reward, I loaded up the waffle maker and topped my second-breakfast with whipped cream, sprinkles, m&ms and those little cookie crumbles—slathering on chocolate syrup until only thin strips of waffle peeked through.

I brought my humble lunch to a shady spot outside. The sky was bright blue. Sunny with a light breeze. And best of all, it was quiet. The first bite was pure bliss. The salmon was lightly seared with just a hint of citrus. I was all alone, and there was no one and nothing stopping me from enjoying my—

"Hello there, darling." A low voice drawled.

An alpha was staring down at me. He was attractive.

Why did all these fucking men have to be so damn hot? It was starting to get annoying.

Buttery blond hair, tossed about like he'd gone for a leisurely sail on his pleasure ship before arriving on land to talk to the common folk. A jawline sharp enough to cut a lady's panties straight off. Eyes that were obnoxiously blue, shimmering like rays of light as they pierced through ocean waves. Deep enough to make me want to jump right in.

Wait, no—I did not want to dive into anything. I had a test to study for. I had online classes. More importantly, I had my lunch to devote all my love and focus on.

I had a huge bite of salmon in my mouth. I couldn't say anything to stop him from sitting down at the table across from me.

I swallowed down my salmon and gulped down water to clear my throat. I was about to tell him off when I was hit by his scent.

Chocolate raspberry.

But not just any chocolate raspberry.

Dark velvety chocolate, his rich and smooth scent wrapped all around me. Decadent and luxurious. Pierced through with a burst of tart raspberry, so sweet and luscious it practically had me moaning.

His scent was pouring through every inch of me. Flooding me until I was drowning.

Yes… Goddamn. I would drown for you.

It had me licking my lips in a way that had nothing to do with finishing my lunch.

Wait. Wait.

Fuck, what was happening?

I did not lick at the scent of alphas, no matter how delicious *this* one happened to smell.

Oh, no. Was this a…

I stared into the eyes of the alpha. He was staring at me wide eyed, with his nostrils flared, and his jaw dropped. I could tell from the dazed look in his eyes that he was sensing this too. He wasn't just any random hot guy. He was my *scent match.*

I cleared my throat.

"Right then. This interview is over."

I grabbed my phone, ready to text my brother. Let him

know that I had found someone perfect, and that he should have the guy join ASAP.

I got to my feet, then stared longingly at the table, biting my lip at the sight of my full plate of food. My immediate getaway meant that I'd have to leave it all behind. It might even be more polite to throw it out.

A not so small part of me was devastated at the thought of having to throw away my delicious lunch after just one measly bite.

"Darling, what are you doing?"

Damn it, I should have just left the salmon... but the waffles. Who left behind a perfectly perfect plate of waffles? Could I have run off with it?

No, that was stupid. Running with waffles was way too sticky. I had to focus. This was like a legit emergency.

"I'm not..." I took a deep breath, realizing that I had raised my voice. "I'm not your darling."

He frowned, shaking his head.

He'd better not say it out loud.

"You're my scent match."

...he said it... out loud.

I wanted to roll my eyes. At who? I don't know. Him. Myself. The whole freaking world, for giving me strenuous academic expectations that I decided to add more classes to... then to top it all off with just a pinch of destiny. With a freaking scent match.

I didn't need a scent match right now. I had class and quizzes, and a very promising career as a secretary in a small business on the line.

He leaned in closer to me, and his blue eyes turned serious.

"I don't think I've ever smelled anything better in my entire life."

Ah. In order for my scent match to believe that I smelled

amazing, he had to be crazy. Of all the omegas I'd met, I had literally the worst scent.

"You don't have to tease me about it, I know what I smell like."

"What? You smell fucking amaz—"

"I smell boring."

Some of the omegas were walking around rocking scents like decadent tobacco and choco musk. Twilight whisky and caramel mocha. Hinoki wood. Bergamot. Oakmoss and vetiver. Tiger orchid. Scents that were spicy and opulent.

Then there was me.

My scent was vanilla.

Vanilla. How incredibly *basic* was that?

Not even vanilla and something else, like coffee. Or even vanilla with another basic scent like rose. It's like somebody ordered the most generic scent for an omega in the whole world and decided to hand it off to me. What did that say about me?

I didn't want to think about it. I had enough problems already.

My scent was *literally* vanilla.

You can't get any more—boring basic bitch—than that.

I mean, I never thought that I was going to go off and fight crime, and take down terrorist plots, and save all of democracy and modern society like my parents all literally did... but the universe didn't have to make it so clear that it wasn't going to happen.

He was pursing his lips like he wanted to say more, but was thinking better of it. Leaving it. For now.

"The other guys are going to be super excited to meet you."

Oh. Hell. No.

I'd forgotten that in order for there to be a scent match, they must have already started the process of pack formation, and wanted to join in with my brother's pack. But the minimum number of guys for a pack was three.

Three guys?

That was like three penises. Where were all those fucking penises expecting to go?

Because it wasn't going to be in me.

I wasn't going to be responsible for getting three peens off. It all sounded like way too much work. How the fuck was I even supposed to get off myself, if I had to focus on three guys at the same time? I wasn't built to do three things at the same time.

What if there were already more than three? Four guys? I didn't even have that many available orifices. Where were they all going to go? Like under me? Over me? Top right and to the side. I didn't want to have to make a map to delicately arrange where all these fuckers were going to go. I didn't want to do fucking math, and *thinking* while having sex.

Nope. No. Not happening.

I had to nip this in the bud. Shut it all down before it was too late.

None of these assholes came here because they wanted me anyway. They shouldn't be my problem. They wouldn't be my problem—Titus put me up to this nonsense. He could fucking deal with getting me out of it.

They wanted to be a pack with my gorgeous brother. Fine. They could have that. Because you know who those fuckers were going to have a chance with?

Not this bitch.

Not Chloe.

CHAPTER 7
KAIN

I THOUGHT I'd prepared for Titus's strange second interview with his sister, but I don't think that anything in my life could have fully prepared me for what had gone down on this random Tuesday afternoon in the Institute cafeteria.

Was there anything that could have prepared me to meet with her?

Chloe Stryker.

She was fucking gorgeous.

Yes, my pack mates had agreed that we wanted to get into Titus Stryker's pack, like many others. Yes, it was in part because of his legacy, and the job prospects that had been lined up...

But to be perfectly honest, there was one little fact that *might* have factored in a bit more than all of that.

Titus Stryker was built like a god.

He was obscenely perfect. It wasn't exaggerating to say that he put the Vitruvian man to shame. If Titus wanted to get into a lucrative modeling career, he could have a contract tomorrow. Honestly, his face belonged on the bottle of every high end perfume. On cereal boxes. On the packaging for all of my boxers and any other unmentionables.

His divine body was like a renaissance sculpture perfected.

I'd been anything but close to being properly prepared for a meeting with his *sister*.

She had a beauty that sort of snuck up on you.

Something about those long lashes of hers, and the delicate splatter of freckles across her nose.

While Titus might have had the kind of gorgeous face that was so overtly handsome, it was as if someone walked straight up to you and smacked you upside the head with his sex appeal…

Chloe had a sweetness that was so subtle and sneaky that it managed to slip through your pores without you noticing. Not until she was already swimming in your bloodstream straight into your beating heart. Making it pound all the harder for her.

She had the girl-next-door kind of appeal that managed to sink somewhere deep into my soul… until without even noticing it, somewhere in the course of a three minute conversation, something shifted within me. Until she somehow pierced straight into the center of all of my motivation. All of my plans for my pack. For my life.

Which didn't even make any fucking sense. I barely knew the girl. She could be a straight up psycho. She could force us all to delete all of our female contacts off our phones (including mothers and cousins) and call us satanic murderers if we didn't instantly switch to becoming level five vegans. Or she could be like an actual psychopath. I'd heard about them sneaking into packs and causing all sorts of trouble for people.

Before this conversation, I was idly curious if my pack could join up and expand. Were we enough to be a part of the Stryker pack? Honestly, I was mildly annoyed that we would have to jump through a bunch more hoops. That was on top of all the formal meetings and paperwork that the Institute already expected from the alphas.

That was all before I'd caught her scent.

I'd never dared to find my scent match.

I'd read all the news articles on it and ran the numbers. I knew the likelihood that I would be able to just bump into my scent match without help from the Institute's Valentine Division (which was honestly kind of stupidly expensive. I mean, you can't put a price on love… but boy did the guys in charge at the Institute like to upsell it).

But I digress.

Chloe smelled divine.

Sweet. Rich. Syrupy. Creamy.

Her scent was sugar cookies in winter and a hug after a hard day. Her scent was everything light and heavenly. Like being all wrapped up in a thick cloud of comforting softness.

More than anything, her scent reminded me of the best flavors within everything. The essence of sweetness. The luxurious cream within the coffee. The frosting on the birthday cake. With smokey notes that were slightly floral and spicy sweet.

Hers was the scent that gave life to all other flavors. The one flavor that gave texture and life to so many others. Arguably, it was simply the best flavor.

Vanilla.

But it was the way that her scent managed to wrap its way around me… not like a vice but a warm embrace. If a scent could be a fucking sign post, hers was neon bright and vibrating. Pointing straight down at this beautiful slip of a girl. Letting me know that she was the source of all of my future happiness. All of my joys. The mother of my mother-fucking children.

Her scent was home.

My scent match.

She was currently staring at me like I was the shit that the dog dragged in. Smeared across her newly mopped floors, after a hard day of cleaning.

"You're here to talk to me because you want to get into a pack with my brother?"

"Well, I was, but obviously—"

"I will send him the best fucking recommendation that you have ever seen. Don't worry, you'll get into his pack. You will bond with him, and we'll never speak of this again."

I had to pick my jaw up from where it had fallen somewhere down on the floor. Somehow, the two of us got our wires crossed. The only thing that was stopping my heart from tumbling out of my chest and breaking apart into little pieces, was the look of pure disappointment on her face.

Not that it was pointed at me. It was pointed at her food.

What? She didn't want to leave her waffle to get away from me?

Whatever. My baby girl could be sad about leaving a perfectly good waffle behind. It gave me an opening.

I just needed a couple of minutes with her. Just enough to figure out why she was staring at me like I'd just punted a kitten like a football while personally taking a dump on all of her hopes and dreams.

The combination of her scent, and her lovely appeal, had me rock hard. I was sitting at the table so it wasn't noticeable, but Chloe was staring at me like she wanted me to leave. If I got up she was going to notice it.

I was still staring at her and... was my mouth hanging open the entire time I'd been plotting and thinking? Goddamn it.

"Screw your brother."

"Exactly, that is the idea," Chloe muttered.

Damn her obnoxiously hot brother, fucking this up for me without even being here.

"No. Fuck fucking him. I don't fucking want him." He was nothing compared to Chloe. The moment that scent bond snapped into place, it was like Titus Stryker no longer existed.

"Really?" Her tone was drowning in skepticism. "All my spare time for the past week has been taken over by alphas desperate for my brother. The only reason we are even talking is because you're trying to get into his pants. Don't even bother trying to deny it."

"I want you."

She didn't believe me. The disbelief was as clear on her face as if she had said the words out loud.

If she could take a peek into my mind, the force of my desire would probably scare her off faster than whatever concerns she'd had that I was here for her brother. I could barely even think straight. With the cafeteria full of rich foods, Chloe was here and smelling better than anything I'd seen on any menu. What I wanted to eat more than anything else, was Chloe, thighs spread, right here on this picnic table. Fuck it, in front of everyone, I didn't give a fuck. Just so I could get a taste of that cream in her dripping pussy, and see if it was as sweet as the rest of her scent that was threatening to over-power me.

Her scent was driving me wild. Pushing me to do something I'd regret. Something that could make us lose her forever.

But what could I say that would make her mine? Now when she was glaring at me. When it was clear that she wanted to run?

She belonged with us. To me and my pack.

But for some reason, I could see the unease clear across each of her features.

"It's nothing personal," Chloe said with a glare that suggested it was definitely personal, "but I don't have time for a pack right now."

She took a deep breath and something in my heart dropped.

Unbelievable. She was not going to just—

"I, Chloe Stryker, officially reject you as my scent match."

Ah. So it took me approximately two minutes to annoy my scent match enough for her to want to reject us. Forget dying of a broken heart. My pack mates were going to kill me as soon as they found out.

Well, I'd managed to fuck everything up. Which was good. Since it was already fucked, I didn't have to worry about fucking things up. It would either stay the same or miraculously get unfucked.

"No." I sounded like a cocky asshole.

"What do you mean no?"

"I reject your rejection."

"You can't just reject a rejection. Why would you do that?"

"Why would you reject us without even giving us a reason?"

All of the alpha instincts within me were screaming at me to stay. Here. To protect my scent match, even if I had to protect her from my mate herself. Even if I had to haul her over my shoulder like a caveman. Run away with her and claim her. She was our omega.

I kind of wanted to pull some toxic shit, like growling at her. Tell her that we weren't done… because she was mine. That I would personally castrate, eviscerate or maybe just emasculate any other man who came close. Who dared to even breathe too close to the girl who's scent was my match.

Guys as hot as Titus could probably pull that off. Even though it was like… kinda misogynistic? More than a bit misogynistic. More like some of it was illegal. Like something that could end in criminal charges and a little bit of jail time if you weren't sexy enough to get away with it…

Speaking of her family, her dads and most of her brothers were pretty built. Strong enough to kill every member of my pack eight or nine times over if we hurt a single hair—no, not even—a single split-end on Chloe's perfect little head.

I was her scent match… and currently just staring at her like I had a screw loose. More than that, like I was completely unhinged.

"I'm not asking for you to accept us, you don't even know anything about us. All I'm asking is that you give us a chance."

"Fine." Chloe abruptly speared her waffle like it was threatening to come back to life and escape off her plate. "So here is how this is going to go. I am busy. I have a demanding academic course load on top of this stupid interviewing task for my brother…"

My scent match wanted to prove herself? Academically? I knew that they assigned homework at the Institute, but I'd never been under the impression that the teachers actually ever expected their omega charges to do all of it. Or any of it, really.

Shit. Focus. My scent match might be accepting my rejection of her rejection. I had to keep my head in the game.

"I will give your pack a chance… " Chloe might have said the words begrudgingly, but a weight I hadn't even noticed lifted off my heart, "but only as long as you aren't fucking up my studies. As soon as you piss me off, we're done. Do you understand me?"

I nodded. I would have agreed to anything, as long as it meant I still had a chance with her. To be perfectly honest, I had to have her. I wanted her. Now. To haul her back into our beds. To show her everything that I couldn't quite put into words. How we would be so good together. That my body was made to please her.

All I had to do was seduce her around her rigorous academic course-load.

Wait…

I'd heard about the kind of *academics* that omegas worked on at the Institute.

Okay then. I held back a smirk that was not going to win me any favors.

Maybe I could find a way to make this work... show her a whole new *learning* experience.

CHAPTER 8
CHLOE

Emmanuel, the alpha currently at my lunch table, was smiling at me way too widely, as if he thought that flirting with me was going to win him points in my brother's favor. Was every single alpha in the whole damn city of New Oxford going to end up sitting at my lunch table and start eye-fucking me? What did a girl need to do to eat her damn sandwich in peace?

Emmanuel checked all the right boxes in terms of tall, dark, and handsome. He had high cheekbones and elegantly sculpted eyebrows that I could imagine him dutifully tweezing with a ruler. But there was just something that I couldn't put my finger on during this interview process. I was pretty good at reading people, but I couldn't quite get a sense of Emmanuel. He'd been perfectly charming so far and said all the right things. But I couldn't ignore the nagging suspicion that something was off about him.

"I can't imagine what an amazing experience it must have been to grow up in the Stryker pack." His smile curved in all the right places, and his dark eyes flashed with interest that at first glance seemed genuine.

Who thought that it was an amazing opportunity to grow up in your own family? It was what it was.

I tried to think back about what part of my upbringing could be considered the glamorous part. The mountains of laundry from a family of twenty-three and counting was pretty majestic. More than a dozen siblings meant more noise. More drama. More dishes in the sink. I mean, my parents were famous, so if Emmanuel wanted to imagine how fabulous it felt for everyone to be in your goddamn business about it every minute of your life, he could do that.

He was honestly really hot... which would make it easier for someone distracted by pretty guys—like my brother Titus—to overlook any signs of bad behavior. Which meant that it was up to me.

It was time for me to go through my Alpha Asshole Red Flag Checklist.

I couldn't do number one of the list, as he hadn't done anything that I could casually comment on. He hadn't been late. There weren't any doors out here in this outdoor picnic area that he hadn't opened for me. So I had to go straight to number two on my list.

Ignore him.

I took another large bite out of the sandwich. Today it was pastrami and provolone on rye. I'd had too many experiences of these meetings completely souring my appetite. This sandwich looked fucking good. I was going to enjoy it, damn it.

The alpha's smile began to fade as I inhaled massive chunks of my lunch in front of him.

Bite after bite, I let the conversation stretch into an uncomfortable silence.

I didn't look his way, though it was clear out of the corner of my eye that he was trying to catch my gaze. He was fidgeting, clearly not happy that I hadn't responded to his perfectly phrased little compliment. It was the third or fourth time that he'd praised me during our conversation. It wasn't quite enough for me to suspect that he was love bombing me, but enough that I couldn't rule it out.

It was barely even two minutes before Emmanuel lost his cool and started fidgeting. By itself, that didn't mean anything. No one liked to be brushed aside in favor of carbs and juicy deli-meat. I could be screwing up a perfectly decent romantic interest for Titus by aggravating this alpha for no reason, but I couldn't ignore my suspicion that something was off.

"Has anyone ever told you that it's rude to ignore people?" Emmanuel snapped.

Ummm… okay?

I stopped myself from blatantly rolling my eyes, leaned back in my chair and took another bite. I focused on the taste of the pastrami, and the gooeyness of the cheese, trying very hard not to let this alpha get in the way of enjoying my meal.

What the hell did he want me to say to him with food crammed into my mouth? I was chewing as fast as I could. It wasn't like I had asked for him or any of the others to start invading my lunches.

I was not willing to *starve* for my brother's future happiness. I might have thought twice about agreeing to help him if I'd known that it was going to come at the price of my lunch time.

Really. Was nothing sacred anymore?

I could spot the exact moment where something shifted in Emmanuel, like a thin cord snapped in half, as he clenched his fists so tight that his knuckles started to get white. He glared at me in a way that was probably meant to be intimidating. It probably would have been… if I didn't have eight brothers. But why was he trying to be intimidating? Did he think that he could scare me into telling Titus to add him to his pack?

"Omega…" The way that Emannuel said my designation… he purred it like he meant to sound seductive. But I couldn't help but hear the undertone of scorn.

He leaned in closer to me, until he was too close, and whispered into my ear, "maybe instead of joining Titus's pack, I'll take you on as my own omega. Someone needs to teach you some manners."

His friendly tone changed, and malice slithered into his every word.

There was something about the way he kept a perfect smile frozen on his face as he spewed out his hatred, that made a chill go down my spine.

Emmanuel was hiding something really nasty behind his perfectly good looks and charm.

He was looking at me with his too handsome face, like he wanted to dig his claws into me and hook me deeper, until I couldn't escape him.

Yeah… about that. I didn't have time to deal with guys with those kinds of issues. I was nobody's therapist.

This wasn't like one of the trashy romance novels I loved to read whenever I could find the time. There was no way that little old me could get involved with someone with serious issues and maladaptive behaviors. I was trying to get my little old degree so that I could go on to work in a respectable office setting. I didn't have the professional tools and the fancy psychology Doctorate to deal with him.

"Hey there, Gorgeous." The voice was way too familiar, despite the fact I'd only heard it once before.

The deep and sultry scent of chocolate hung heavy in the air, as if I was dropped headfirst into a candy store, as my scent match strolled over to my table.

The same smile remained on Emmanuel's face, but now that I recognized him for what he was, it seemed almost stretched thin, with all the warmth sucked out of it.

"The two of us are having a private conversation."

Emmanuel said in a confident tone that left no room for argument.

Except that I'd had enough of hanging around alphas with questionable mental statuses and wasn't afraid of being just a little rude to get the fuck out.

"Hey, yourself," I put a little more warmth into my greeting than I actually felt. Definitely more affection, attention and effort than I'd put into Emmanuel at any point. At this point, fuck it. He didn't deserve it.

Emmanuel didn't like that I was paying another alpha attention. He completely turned his back on me, as his aura pierced the air, with an energy that was crackling and unstable. "I said, we're having a private conversation."

Fuck. This.

This was getting way too dramatic. I was just here doing a favor, interviewing all these dramatic ass alphas. I did not ask for them to start getting all testy and belligerent, right in front of my poor half-eaten sandwich.

"Did you still want my help with that professor?" The playful tone in Kain's voice was gone. There was no professor I needed help with. My academic situation was rock solid. But I knew exactly what Kain was really asking: Was this guy bothering you? Do you want my help?

"That sounds great. I have him next period." I grabbed my tray, swiftly rising to my feet and away from the table before Emmanuel even realized what was going on. I was going to get the hell out of this conversation, and far from Emmanuel.

"This isn't over," Emmanuel hissed.

With that comment, I did roll my eyes. Whatever he needed to say in order to make him feel better about this situation. Did he think that I was going to become his omega because he got angry and glared at me? Did I look desperate or something?

No, I'd had quite enough from Emmanuel.

I had places to go. Mainly to my class. Brothers to kill...

even if it broke the horny hearts of every single alpha lingering around the Institute. Like seriously, Titus was really asking too much of me. I had a lesson starting in fifteen minutes and I needed to leave now in order to get a seat in the front and center of class. I was not going to let any alpha-hole mess up the solid academic impression I was steadily making on all my teachers.

The last thing I needed was all this male attention right now. There was so much testosterone in the air that it was probably poison at this point, lowering my IQ with every breath I took.

I scarfed down the rest of my sandwich, even though it was way too delicious for that hasty goodbye, and dropped my tray unceremoniously on top of the trash cans furthest from Emmanuel. I let Kain place a hand at the small of my back, helping to hustle me out of the cafeteria area.

I sighed.

It really was too much for these alphas with anger issues to handle when an omega stopped paying attention to them for a few minutes. Did Emmanuel think that omegas were born specifically to worship his stupid little handsome face or something?

Today was turning into too much, and it was barely past noon.

Who would have thought that I would have to add "eat my sandwich" to my Red Flag checklist?

CHAPTER 9
CHLOE

"I ONLY LET you rescue me because that guy is something else." I muttered.

"A tough little darling like you doesn't need rescue," Kain agreed easily. "But that alpha was getting hostile, and there was no reason for you to have to deal with that."

I sighed. Kain was right. I suppose I was being a little ungrateful. If it wasn't for Kain showing up when he did, it would have been rather obnoxious to extricate myself from an alpha who was being rather clingy and unnecessarily aggressive. Or worse, I might have ended up getting to class *late*.

Some alphas just couldn't handle it when a little-bitty omega like me wasn't basically drooling over his every word, desperately lapping up his affection. Not only that, I had apparently committed the unspeakable crime of *eating* instead. I'm sure that if I had spoken to Emmanuel with a dazed expression of rapture, hanging on to his every word like a dumb bimbo, he wouldn't have seen anything wrong with it. He'd probably just taken that attention as his due.

Comparing Kain to *that* was setting the bar too low. Honestly, the bar was all the way on the ground when it came to alpha-holes. But I guess that Kain wasn't that bad.

Since we had scent matched last week, Kain had been around. He'd seen me interviewing the other alphas and never bothered me before. He must have been checking in on me, and noticed that there was something off today.

To be totally honest, I never thought that I would want to be rescued. Every single fairy tale about princesses in towers, rescued from the dragons and witches or whatever was just not my thing. I thought it was all dumb until I was rescued from the humiliation that came from awkward social situations.

"Thank you for getting me out of there."

"If you want to thank me, let me take you out on a date." The smile was back on Kain's face.

Ughh. I was too freaking busy to go out on a date. I had that chapter to read on flavored lubes tonight, and I had to get started on an essay if I wanted to get ahead on my online classes. But I also didn't have time to argue with him. Not if I wanted to get to my favorite spot in the front.

Besides, I did agree to give my scent matches a chance. I guess saving me from a psychopath earned him a date. Maybe just a short one. I could always get ahead on my coursework tomorrow.

"Fine," I agreed, mostly to get him out of my hair.

"You free tonight at seven?"

"Sure," I said, waving him off so I could get to class.

Kain scurried away as if he was leaving before I could change my mind, taking that luxurious dark scent of chocolate away with him.

As soon as I was front and center in the classroom, I took my seat with a sigh. I was the first omega to arrive, getting here even before our professor.

Angling my phone, so that it was hidden behind my mini tower of text-books, I texted my brother.

Me: Emmanuel is a psychopath.

I saw the three dots pop up immediately. He was probably still at lunch.

Titus: Oh, I was worried when you hadn't mentioned any, that you were going to let one sneak into my new pack.

Seriously? I went through all these interviews and he wasn't even going to listen to my warning? Maybe he just thought that I was exaggerating.

Me: Emmanuel is the worst. Literally the worst. Pick anyone but him.

Titus: That's what you said about like every single guy

I couldn't take my eyes off the screen of my phone. The message was getting blurred around the edges as tears got in the way.

Stupid tears. They were probably just stress tears. This was just more stupid shit that I didn't need to deal with. Having my lunch time invaded by alphas. All the homework for my classes at the Institute, and then the college classes I was taking on top of that… It was a lot.

I was literally putting my own dreams for my future at stake to make sure that my stupid-ass brother didn't end up heart-broken with his choice of pack mates, and for what?

My fingers were tapping across the screen and sent a message before I was fully aware of what I'd sent.

Me: You're a douche canoe

I stared at the message. It was a little harsh, but was it wrong? I kinda half wished that there was a way to unsend it.

But at the same time, all of this was my brother's fault for being a douche canoe. Three little dots had already bubbled up on the bottom of the screen. Titus had already seen my accusation of his douchee-ness.

> Titus: Wait. Did that fucker do something to hurt you?

Shit. I typed fast, before my hot-headed brother forwarded the message to my dads and started a riot.

> Me: No

> Me: Just was rude, and aggressive for no reason

Should I tell him about Emmanuel threatening to make me his? Was that even a valid concern? Like I just needed to say no, and that was going to be the end of it.

> Titus: Wait, what about the alpha you met before them? You never said anything about Kain?

Oh, shit.

I hadn't said anything about the guys that I'd scent matched with had I? Originally I was going to give them a stellar report, and make sure that Titus took them into his pack. But, I'd already told them that I'd give them a chance.

Why the fuck did I give them a second chance? It was something about the very confident way that Kain said no, as he tried to hide a look of absolute panic that made me reevaluate. Yes, I might not want to deal with a scent match. But I knew the numbers. I'd heard all about the low probabilities directly from a scientist at the Institute. His lecture kind of felt like a sales pitch to me, since he worked at the Valentine's

Division. Anyway, the important thing was that even though I didn't want a scent match right now, these alphas might not get another chance. Ever.

It wasn't like there was anything visibly wrong with Kain. He was drop-dead gorgeous, nice enough and didn't seem like the kind of guy who would get all weirdly possessive and run off with me into his man-cave or some toxic shit like that. Assuming I wanted to get into a relationship at some point, I guess a scent match wasn't a bad option? It was like the universe creating a giant billboard from the heavens, telling me via scent that these guys would be a compatible match for me. Should I throw that all away for a chance at a quiet desk job?

Damn, I still hadn't answered my brother.

Me: he's okay.

I tried to play it off casually.

I guess that it worked because I didn't hear anything back from him. Not a single peep during the entire lecture on the biology of alpha ruts. I took notes diligently, making sure to get the exact names of the chemical reactions—the epinephrine and cortisol in the adrenal gland. Something about excitatory amino acids that I missed because I was busy googling the correct spelling.

I was jotting down the last few sentences just as class was ending, when I heard the uproar. There were audible gasps coming from my classmates.

I was vaguely worried that there was something serious happening—like a fire, or maybe one of the Beta-terrorist organizations like the Reset.

It was a legitimate concern, as that group did target omegas in their teens and early twenties. For some reason they believed that young omegas would bring about societal collapse… by being sexy or putting on too much lipstick or something.

But then I heard one of my classmates whisper, in a voice totally loud enough for everyone in the room to hear, "I want to have all of his babies."

What the fuck? Why say that?

My gaze snapped up to see the very last person I needed to see right now.

Titus, leaning against the wall, staring right at me.

After weeks of showing my academic potential, I could feel all my effort getting thrown out the window. I was about to be known as the obnoxiously hot alpha's sister.

Great. Just great.

CHAPTER 10
CHLOE

TITUS WAS DRESSED in a shirt and jeans that he somehow managed to look designer, even though I was pretty sure that I remember him throwing it in the shopping cart when we'd been out at Target.

One of my classmates just said that she wanted to have his babies.

If I could hear it then Titus could definitely hear it.

Why? Just why?

Now that I was paying attention, the other omegas didn't look like they were in danger as much as they just low-key wanted to throw themselves at him. Literally throw themselves bodily at him.

Opening my sexual anatomy book, I walked past Titus like I didn't even see him. In my peripheral vision, I noted how his jaw tensed. His longer stride easily matched mine as he followed me out of the class.

As soon as we were alone, I dropped the act and glared at Titus. "What do you want?"

"Your last text was concerning."

Which was the last text? Was it the stuff about Emmanuel?

"That guy, Emmanuel… if I hadn't said anything, how likely would it be for you to put him into your pack?"

"I mean Emmanuel? Well, he seems like a nice guy. He's pretty cute…" Titus just shrugged.

Something within me sank at the realization.

Why was Titus so oblivious?

I wanted to quit this stupid interviewing thing, but did he literally have no idea that he was about to bond with an alpha like *that*? Was he so ready to walk into the loving arms of a backstabbing jerk?

Alpha bonds were no joke. He'd be able to sense those other guy's emotions in his mind all the time… for the rest of his life. I had no idea why these alphas weren't taking mental health into consideration. I couldn't imagine how having a bond with someone with anger issues would impact your happiness.

"Yeah, all the other guys that you sent my way… some of them have been just clueless, or straight up dumb. But Emmanuel? I think that he's a psychopath. No, I mean literally. There's something about him that is definitely off. Like he hides it well, but I think that he could be legitimately evil."

"I don't care about Emmanuel. If you say he's shit, he's shit. I'm not going to bond with him."

I hadn't noticed the tension that had built up in the pit of my stomach until it was suddenly gone. I hadn't noticed how anxious I'd felt about Titus bonding an asshole until just now.

Titus frowned when he noticed me sighing. "Was Emmanuel really being psychotic? Do you want me to get him to apologize?"

I shook my head, trying to dislodge the mental image of Emmanuel's pathetic attempt at saying sorry if he was ever forced to apologize to anyone. He just seemed like the kind of guy who was so convinced that he was right that he would need to consult a written list of different ways to apologize for hurting people. There was no way that he was simply human enough to feel regular emotions and produce the words that sounded even close to empathic. I wasn't up to hearing his bastardized and cheap imitation of sounding like a decent human. It seemed like more effort than it was worth. I didn't have the mental energy to deal with that right now.

"So what's going on with Kain?" Titus crossed his arms as he stared at me with an expression he'd photocopied from Father.

"Uhh…" damn. Titus was not supposed to pick up on that. What happened to him being oblivious? "Why would anything be going on with Kain?"

I did not want my family involved in my relationships before I even figured out what I wanted with these guys. I hadn't even *met* the entire pack. I didn't even know all their *names.*

"Hey," Titus grabbed my shoulders, watching me closely. The look in his eyes was burning, promising vengeance and swift retribution. "Your text said that he's okay. You literally had nothing nice to say about a single one of the alphas that I sent your way. Is he blackmailing you? Tell me what's going on."

Damn, Titus thought that I was actually in danger or something. Well, I couldn't let him think that Kain was using me… but I was kinda hoping to still be able to pawn my scent matches off on him once they started to annoy me.

"Alright, I'll tell you what's up with him. But can you please promise me that you won't tell anyone? I mean no one. Not even our parents."

"Okay?" Titus clenched his jaw. He had to be grinding his teeth—and he knew better than to mess with his teeth after wearing braces for three years when he was in middle school.

Why did he say it as a question? I did *not* mean it as a question.

"Promise me, or I'm not saying a word." I narrowed my eyes at him.

"Okay, fine. I promise. What is it?"

"So Kain ended up being my scent match."

"Oh my God! Chloe," Titus pulled me in for an enthusiastic hug. "That's great!"

"No!" I pulled out of the hug, shaking my head. Did no one ever listen to me? "This is the worst thing that could have happened to me."

"Okay… not great then." Titus frowned, as he tried to wrap his head around the very simple fact that I did not want scent matches. "Are they just not your type? Do you just dislike them or something?"

"I don't know, I haven't even met any of the pack besides Kain, and he's not bad." I crossed my arms across my chest and raised my chin. Just because my brother was stupidly taller than me and older than me did not mean that his points were any more important than mine. He wasn't going to talk me out of my priorities.

"So, what's the problem?"

"I don't want a scent match right now. There are just other things that are more important to me." I knew that the most important thing for my future happiness was *not* dick. I needed to focus on my academics in order to get my dream job.

Titus just stared at me.

I glared right back at him. "What?"

"What do you mean, what? What's more important to you than having a pack? Not just a pack, one with your scent match?"

"What is even the point of a pack of alphas if they aren't going to listen to me!" I rubbed my forehead, trying to soothe away the headache caused by my brother's nonsense. "Just the thing that I've been saying for months. I want to finish my college classes. I want to get my degree."

"You do?" Titus said slowly, in a tone that suggested that I was crazy. "Why do you even want a degree? What are you going to do with it?"

"I'm going to get a respectable job, in a nice quiet office, with no one to bother me. I just want to be left alone to be a productive member of society in peace."

"But they're your scent match," Titus repeated himself as if the words meant something different the second time around.

"I don't know if I want a scent match," I grumbled. "Our parents aren't scent matches, and they are all perfectly happy."

Titus just stared at me, as if *I* was the crazy one.

"The one brother that I met was actually a pretty decent guy. He'd be a solid addition to your own pack." Whatever. I wasn't actually sure if I wanted to give them up, but it was still a win for the guys if they got to hook up with Titus.

"Yeah, no little sis. I am not so hard up for alphas that I'm going to steal your scent matches in order to make a decent pack."

Well there went my back up plan. My get-rid-of-the-scent-matches quick plan was completely trashed in the course of one short conversation.

Titus was really leaving me no choice but to spend time with sexy men that were falling over themselves to please me. When was I supposed to do that? Who had time for desperate and gorgeous alphas? It was like no one other than me was taking my academics seriously.

None of this was fair.

CHAPTER 11
KAIN

"HOW DO I LOOK?" I'd changed my outfit three times already, trying to find the perfect balance of clothing that looked well put-together without trying too hard—I wanted it to look like I hadn't made a mini mountain of rejected clothes in a pile on my bed, even though I clearly *had*.

"I don't know why you're stressing about it. She's our scent match. She's going to be attracted to us." My twin, Sabien, was sprawled lazily on top of the rejected pile of outfits, like an omega in a clothing nest.

"Yeah, but this girl isn't like other girls."

"Isn't that just a thing that girls say... when they are just like other girls but want to feel special, by acting allergic to the color pink or something?" Sabien stretched out, making himself more comfortable and putting deeper wrinkles in all of my clothes.

"No, I mean that she practically rejected us off the bat," *and who the hell does that to their scent match?* "She's drowning in alpha attention because of some scheme her brother cooked up. Most omegas would be dying of happiness, and our girl is just dying inside."

"That's probably just because she had the misfortune of

meeting *you* first." Sabien said it with a completely straight face, no smirking or anything. He actually *meant* that I was the problem. "You should let me get the first crack at her. Hell, set her up on a date with Brutus. He'll have her melting into a pile of happy omega goo in twenty minutes flat."

"Absolutely not." I love my brother, I really do, but sometimes he is the world's biggest idiot. Between the three of us, Brutus was the most likely to have Chloe screaming for the hills. "We don't want to overwhelm her." She was already acting enough like a cornered animal. *I* would be the one to meet her, because between the three of us, I was arguably the least offensive alpha. Besides, she had already met me. I didn't want to throw anything new at her when everything was still up in the air. We were going to treat our scent match with the utmost care.

Sabien and Brutus had basically forced me to be the pack lead. Obviously, my twin shouldn't be in charge of anything, but when I'd asked Brutus, he'd laughed in my face and told me to deal with that paperwork shit. In his words, he only wanted to be in charge of the fucking.

Well, I had somehow ended up in charge, and I was not going to fuck this up for the rest of the pack. Besides the fact that the others would never speak to me again if I messed this up, they put me in charge for a reason.

Now all I had to do was un-fuck everything up.

"Whatever." Sabien waved me off, not paying attention. "Just make sure to give her my number. I'll set up a date with her and fix whatever mess you make tonight."

I turned away so that Sabien couldn't see me rolling my eyes at him. I was just about ready to head out for my date, when it hit me. "Wait. You said that Chloe should go out with Brutus first. Does that mean that you two have stopped—"

"Hell, no." My twin cut me off. He burrowed deeper into my clothing nest. His voice was slightly muffled by the fabric.

He looked ready to take a nap. "But just cuz I'm pissed at him, doesn't mean I'm not ready to use him."

Damn. I thought that the feud between the two of them would have eased up. They'd never fought about anything before. Honestly, the two of them had been so inseparable I'd almost felt a little left out in my own pack. But now, nothing. Both Sabien and Brutus had shut down the pack bond hard, so I could only get glimpses of what they were feeling.

After getting used to sensing their emotions all the time, it was getting rather lonely in my own head.

I didn't have time to think about it, not if I wanted everything to go perfect tonight.

I stood outside of the omega dorm buildings, waiting for Chloe.

Tonight was about showing her that having three men catering to her every desire was somewhat more fun than piles of essays and a rigid academic course load.

That had to be more pleasurable than homework? Right? I mean, unless piles of paperwork and academic mastery was some kind of a kink? That wasn't the reason why most people went to college and got their degrees, it wasn't like a diploma could stroke egos better than a lover in bed.

Before I even saw her, the scent of vanilla swirled thick in the air, hitting me with the sweet essence of milkshakes, custards, and cakes. Smooth and luxurious, like silk on my tongue, beckoning me to come closer, and get another taste.

Her eyes locked on mine flashing with heat, as she stepped out of the dorms. I wish that the heat in her eyes was due to desire, but it seemed like she was just annoyed with me. Even pissed off, she was stunning.

Her lovely eyes, surrounded by dark lashes, flashed with piercing intelligence. Chloe was tall for an omega. Normally she wore jeans, or sweatpants with a hoodie to class, but for our date she'd changed into a knitted dress, showing off her toned calves and delicate ankles.

This was the first time I'd seen my girl without her stack of textbooks—before Chloe, I hadn't even been aware of the fact that omegas even had textbooks for their classes. At least none of the other girls around campus carried them around with them. Without the books, Chloe was like a completely different person.

"Alright, the food at this place better be good," Chloe muttered. "I barely got to enjoy lunch with that psychopath breathing down my throat."

"Yeah, they have food there."

My vague answer piqued Chloe's attention. She looked at me more closely, a smile tugging up the corners of her lips. "Wait, you aren't taking me to a restaurant? Where are we going?"

"No, where's the fun in that?" I twirled my car keys around my pointer finger.

I wasn't going to waste my one chance to impress Chloe by doing something as basic as taking her out on a date to some restaurant. Besides, from what I'd seen, Chloe had been hard at work everyday, completely focused. All work and no play.

I was so looking forward to playing with her.

Chloe did not look impressed when I pulled into the parking lot of the New Oxford aquarium. She crossed her arms across her chest, leaning back into her seat. "The sign says they close in five minutes."

"Which'll be perfect for us." I hurried out of the car, hustling over to her side to open the door for her. "No lines. No screaming kids. The whole place will be just for us."

"You want us to break into the aquarium? When I'm wearing a dress?" Chloe leaned further into the car as if she was afraid that I was going to drag her out and force her to commit to a life of depravity and crime.

"Nah, I know the owners." I opened the door wider and smiled in what I hoped was a confident way.

Chloe raised an eyebrow, as she exited the car.

Alright. That was a start. At least I had her curious. I'd been half afraid that she was going to scoff at the whole idea and demand that I take her back to the Institute.

Frank was working at the reception desk, frowning down at a computer screen. "Sorry, we close in four—oh, it's you," he dropped the professional voice as soon as he looked up and saw me. Frank waved me in. "If you see Slippy, can you email Tom? He got out of his tank again. Haven't seen him since noon."

"Yeah, will do." I agreed, making a mental note to check the area for any wandering octopus.

As I led Chloe through the exhibits, she slowed down, staring wide-eyed as we neared the jellyfish exhibit. So far so good. She didn't even seem to notice the screaming toddlers that weren't ready to go and their exhausted parents who looked just about ready to pull out their own hair. One mother turned bright red as her kid started screeching like a pterodactyl as he refused to leave. I mentally patted myself on the back for thinking of bringing Chloe after hours.

I led Chloe straight to Undersea Eats, the restaurant that had seating in the open ocean tunnel, with panoramic views of the sharks and sea-turtles. It also had some of the best food in the area. I wasn't just talking about the aquarium, but also better food than half the restaurants in town. My scent match did treat her meal times like they were sacred. To treat her like the goddess she was, I'd have to give her the best meal offerings.

"Do you see anything you like? The salmon's really good, as are the burgers." I pointed each item out on the menu.

"Uhh, salmon?" Chloe said it like it was a question, but I'd seen her eating salmon loads of times.

"Be right back with your order, darling." I stepped into the back.

It only took a few minutes of sweet talking to the head Chef and listening to him grumbling about having to clean the counters again to get him to make two of the best plates that Underwater Eats had to offer.

I was rewarded when Chloe's eyes brightened as she got a glimpse of the dinner. Chef Thompson plated everything extra fancy when I told him the food was for my date, not my brother. The salmon was perfectly seared and looked buttery soft and perfect. I'd gotten the usual for myself: surf and turf, steak medium rare with the loaded mashed potatoes on the side. I'd never found another restaurant with mashed potatoes as fluffy. I didn't even know that potatoes could become this cloud-like and creamy.

Chloe dug into her salmon with gusto, as if it was going to get up and swim away if she ignored it for too long, joining the rest of the schools in the tank surrounding us. She watched the sea life swimming above us with wide eyes, and yelped when one of the sharks swam right over our table.

"What kind of shark is that?" Chloe pointed, leaning away as if she was worried that the little guy would be able to swim through the glass and come after her. It was a *Sphyrna tiburo*, commonly known as the bonnethead shark, but I wasn't about to out myself as a nerd.

"Yeah, that's a gray one with a weird head." I winked at her, and Chloe rolled her eyes at me, though she didn't seem like she was pissed. "Sharks with dinner aren't what you expected?"

Chloe raised an eyebrow at me. "Well, I'm staring at fish as I eat a fish."

"Is that putting you off your salmon?"

"Hell, no." Chloe took another large bite to emphasize her point. "This is really good."

"What about the company?" I leaned back in the chair,

giving Chloe a good view. Might as well, after trying on seven different shirts, to find one that showed off the muscles in my chest while not appearing like I was trying to flaunt them.

"Not bad." Chloe smirked, making a show of looking me up and down. She totally picked up on how I was flexing as I tried to work out whether she was attracted to me. "I mean, if you want to know my sexual preferences… I like men. I'm a little attracted to women… but to be a hundred percent accurate, I'm mostly attracted to fictional characters in books more than real people of any gender."

"Ah. So my competition is a shirtless Fabio." I smirked at her, enjoying her flirty teasing.

"More like a millionaire werewolf, who is also in the mafia."

"Who could forget those very sexy… werewolf mafia men? Right."

"What about you? Did you want a larger pack?"

I heard what Chloe wasn't saying. Were we disappointed that we ended up with her as a scent match instead of in a pack with her brother? Did she think that my pack somehow still wanted Titus? That we weren't attracted to her?

Damn Titus Stryker and his stupidly beautiful body. He was totally cock-blocking my whole pack right now.

"Are you asking if my pack needs a mafia man who turns into a rich wolf?"

Chloe smiled, caught off guard. "Be serious."

"I just want you." Under the table, I clenched my hands together briefly, before releasing them. My fingers were aching with the need to touch her.

She shook her head. "You wanted my brother. Meeting me was just an afterthought."

"Titus has elite connections. It was too good of an opportunity to pass up. I would hate it if my pack never even applied. That was our chance to push our limits. See what the three of us are capable of. But besides that, I thought that my pack had everything I needed. Until I met you."

Chloe ducked her head. Was that red creeping up along her cheeks? Did I make my scent match blush? *"Jesus. I didn't even ask the other alphas what their intentions were with my brother. I just assumed that they all just wanted to get in his pants."*

"To be fair, that is a fair assumption." I had to steer the conversation away from her obnoxiously good-looking brother and back where it belonged. On *her.* "Are you happy with your classes at the Institute?"

If I was a different kind of alpha, more of a smooth talker, maybe I could have maneuvered this conversation with my charisma and sex appeal. But alas, I was just me. Besides, I wanted to get to know Chloe a little better.

I had to believe that being authentically myself wasn't going to fuck everything up. Chloe was our scent match, that meant that there was something inside of us that made us compatible. If I couldn't be myself around her, what even was the point of having a scent match?

"I think at some level it's important. If omegas knew nothing about their own biology, it could be rather hard to navigate their impulses. Can you imagine the kind of chaos that would unfold if an omega just tried scenting random household appliances? Her instincts could make her scent mark her microwave or the blender, and then her alphas would start hoarding those appliances. How would anyone be able to even eat a decent meal?"

I nodded. That made perfect sense. If you looked at it that way it wasn't entirely bad for omegas to learn a little about the biology that drove them instead of getting sucked in by all of it.

"So, you enjoy the basic curriculum? Would you ever want to join one of the academies?"

"Absolutely not. I'm not in love with studying, it's all just a means to the end."

"What would that end be? What do you dream about?"

"Honestly?" Chloe drew herself up and stared at me with a challenge in her eye. Mentally I drew myself up too. This was it. She was revealing to me her deepest, darkest desires. All I had to do was be supportive and let her know that it was all going to work out. "I want to get my degree so that I can get a quiet desk job."

I nodded slowly. It sounded like a good first step to a solid career. A position in an office was a realistic entry job for someone as motivated as Chloe.

"What would you want to do next? Move up the corporate ladder? Do you eventually want to be a manager?"

"No, that's basically it. I want to be like a secretary."

I held myself back from asking *why*. I wasn't stupid enough to shit all over her dreams, even if her dreams weren't what I expected. Though I had honestly never heard of anyone who wanted to be a secretary before as their dream job. That didn't mean that there was anything necessarily wrong with wanting that.

A powerful and sexy queen bee like Chloe was the kind of person that could have anything that her heart desired. That little heart of hers desired a desk job.

Okay. That was fine. We could work with that.

CHAPTER 12
CHLOE

I DON'T KNOW why I expected a date with Kain to be normal. Since I was desperate for some peace and quiet in my chaotic life, it was obvious that my scent match would pull off a series of crazy stunts. But honestly, I wasn't expecting for this to be so much fun.

Kain had that grin on his face that I couldn't help finding adorable, while letting the penguins out of their enclosure, reassuring me that he could get them back with promises of sardines easily enough.

"It's good for them." He'd shrugged.

I raised an eyebrow at him, communicating wordlessly. *Really?*

"No one should spend all their time caged. It's healthy to get out, shake things loose every once in a while."

So that was how I found myself surrounded by penguins that were waddling all around me. They were little chubby birds wearing sleek tuxedos, like they had been all invited to a fancy party with good food.

We passed by a rainforest section, surrounded by tanks that had thick gnarly tree roots, with enormous fish swimming under them. The penguins waddled straight up to the glass and tried to take a bite out of them. Which luckily wasn't happening. I wasn't sure if it was even good for the penguins to be eating fish so far out of their habitat. Surely it would give them indigestion or something.

There were seven of them. I knew it, because I kept on neurotically counting them whenever we walked to a new area of the aquarium.

Kain didn't seem to have any problems corralling the penguins around. Obviously, it was something he had done before, as he would let out a little whistle when one of them got too far, and then the chubby little birds would go running back towards him excitedly, like he was their favorite fish dealer.

Kain brought them to a theater within the aquarium. Then, he went into the back and put on a short film about penguins. A narrator, with a deep British voice, started droning on about the natural habitat of the Humboldt penguins, as the ones we were taking on a walk tried and failed to hop all over the theater seats.

I'm not going to lie, I went on this date expecting nothing but free food and looking for any excuse to turn down my scent matches once and for all. I could remember each and every one of my excuses, how I didn't have enough time, that I didn't have the mental bandwidth to deal with a pack of men in the first place, how I didn't need scent matches to find my dream job...

Each of those excuses sort of faded away every time that Kain looked back in the midst of doing something ridiculously crazy, and winked at me.

Like right now, he had a line of penguins following him out of the theater, back to their enclosures like a group of slow moving but enthusiastic puppies.

I couldn't help it. There was something in his ridiculously handsome face, something about his casual confidence, that had me melting.

Just a little bit.

Maybe. Just, maybe… it wouldn't hurt to give these guys a *little bit* more of a chance.

I mean, what did I have to lose if it turned out he was a red flagged asshole after all? I could always break up with them later.

CHAPTER 13

KAIN

CHLOE SHIVERED AS SOON as we stepped into Mochi's enclosure, and I took that as a sign to pull off my jacket and hand it to her. I immediately shoved down any weird thoughts about how I was getting my scent on her. The last thing that I wanted to do was to screw up the entire date by acting too eager, like I was planning on huffing the fabric as soon as I got it back from her.

"Are you sure that it's okay that we're doing this?" Chloe asked as we approached the icy water of the tank.

"Yeah, we're providing some extra enrichment."

The outer wall was carved out of rocks that extended up to the lip of the tank. It seemed like it was pulled from another world, as the reflection of water rippled across the stone surface, and the turquoise depths seemed to glow.

There was something calming about being here, even as the cold chilled all the way through me. The thought always struck me that just outside these walls, we were surrounded by the city, with all of its traffic and stress, all the trappings of civilization. It felt like none of that had ever existed here.

This had always been my favorite place. But somehow it

felt like more as I observed Chloe looking around the enclosure, taking everything in with brand new eyes.

I stood by the edge of the water and crooned, "Hey pretty lady."

Mochi popped her white bulbous head out of the water and chirped a greeting at me.

"Why's she all alone?" Chloe stood behind me, but leaned forward, watching everything with wide-eyed amazement.

"Mochi usually stays with the others, but she's super pregnant right now." I showed Mochi the bag filled with her art supplies. "Do you want to make a painting for Chloe?"

My lovely little beluga friend bobbed her head up and down with enthusiasm.

Mochi opened her mouth wide, and I handed over her paintbrush. I held a canvas out, while Mochi jerked her head back and forth, expressing her creativity in strokes and slashes. Honestly, the work was no van Gogh, but she was a whale, painting with her mouth using a brush covered in duct tape. Anyway, we all had our talents. I wasn't one to point out Mochi's artistic flaws. Besides, it looked perhaps slightly better than something a human toddler could whip together.

"That's brilliant Mochi," I lied, as I took the brush back from her. I was grinning at her work as if it was actually a magnificent piece of art. Well I wasn't about to hurt my favorite whale's feelings now, was I?

I patted her forehead, and stroked along Mochi's cheeks. "Who's the sweetest girl?"

Mochi twirled around in the water, like a blubbery ballerina and then opened her mouth expectantly.

"I don't have any treats for you, not today."

Mochi trilled. I didn't realize before today that a friendly little whale could sound so betrayed.

"I'm sorry! You're on a special diet. I promise that—" I had to jerk out of the way, as an indignant Mochi sprayed me with water… and ended up soaking my scent match's shoes instead.

Shit.

Which is how I found myself outside of the woman's bathroom, holding a whale painting and questioning all of my life choices.

Though Chloe laughed about it, and the whale spray only reached her shoes and just the bottom of her dress, I'd seen her viciously tear apart the alphas interested in her brother for far less of an indiscretion.

Fuck.

What was worse, was that before I managed to piss off the pregnant whale, I thought that there had been a moment, a spark of something real and fragile starting to form between Chloe and me. Too bad that I probably managed to squash it all with whale spit. There was no way I could have fucked up this date any worse.

And that's when I heard Chloe's panicked screaming.

I ran into the woman's bathroom, immediately ignoring the fact that it was much better smelling than the men's room. I sprinted over to Chloe, hauling her against my chest, ready to fight whatever it was that had her terrified.

"What is it?" I couldn't get Chloe to calm down. She was panicked, clutching on to my shirt hard. So close that I could feel her blood pounding as I held her.

She was staring at a mass of writhing tentacles moving across the glass in the bathroom mirror. I could see how that might be rather jarring, if she was going to fix her lipstick, looked at her reflection and saw a sea creature in its place.

A rather large, bright red octopus was sliding across the mirror, his suckers pulled himself across the glass, as he sneaked across the facility in the night.

"Oh that's Mr. Slippy, our resident escape artist." I pulled

Chloe closer against me. Her entire body was shaking, so I wrapped my arms around her, rubbing soothing patterns against her arms. "You're alright." I murmured into her ear. "I got you."

Chloe tore her gaze away from Mr. Slippy, who was already all the way off the window, pulling himself toward the drainage pipes, and managing to squeeze his fat body through the vertical slats. I swear that the little bugger recognized me. He always seemed to move faster whenever I was around.

I wasn't too worried about him. Mr. Slippy knew how to get back into his tank as easily as he could get out of it. He'd be back in the morning, in time for his breakfast.

No, I had more important things to worry about than that wayward octopus.

Like the fact that Chloe was closer to me than ever before. I was holding her in my arms and she was clutching me like I was her last hope.

Chloe seemed to recognize it at the same moment as me, she gasped and looked up into my face, though she didn't try to move away.

She was looking into my eyes, like she was reading all the secrets of the universe, like she was desperate to know what I was thinking.

The joke was on her, the moment that I saw her long eyelashes, the slight curve of her cheekbones, those plush lips up close... every thought burned out of my mind.

Chloe was so gorgeous. So fucking gorgeous, and gazing up at me like she wanted me.

I leaned down and kissed her.

The moment that my mouth touched hers, it felt as though every inch of my skin was on fire. It was so good, so impossibly good.

Chloe kissed me back, moving her luscious lips against mine, creating a soft friction that was out of this world. I tightened my arms around her. I wanted to freeze this moment and live in it forever. Sultry vanilla was thick in the air, sweet and creamy and burrowing into me, sinking through my pores and igniting my blood.

Once we broke apart, Chloe was looking up at me with a hint of a smile in her eyes. She watched me as if the two of us had just shared a brilliant secret.

"Shouldn't you, I don't know, go after him?" She nodded toward the drainage hole.

"Can't fit down the pipe."

"That's too bad."

"Yeah."

I nodded, with a very serious expression on my face. Though I felt like everything was in a daze. Everything was so perfect it didn't even feel real. What was I talking about? Something about an octopus?

Chloe stood up on her tiptoes and kissed me again.

CHAPTER 14
KAIN

"YOUR DATE WENT WELL?" Sabien asked. He was perched on the counter, lounging against the kitchen cabinets, knobs and everything, though there was no way that leaning like that was actually comfortable.

All I could think about was Chloe's lips. They were the lips of a siren, drawing me in. Impossibly soft, she was silk against my mouth. What wouldn't I give for another taste? They were the most delicious, the most dangerous lips in the world.

I nodded in reply, blissed out.

It really went well. There was no arguing that. At the start of the date, Chloe had been on the cusp of rejecting our pack. I'd left Chloe with stars in her eyes and a promise to see us again.

Sabien nodded in approval. "Where did you take her?"

"The Aquarium." I turned to my brother, ready to give him the good news, how Chloe had a fantastic time. That she wanted to see more of us.

But I stopped when I saw Sabien's expression like he was choking on a lemon.

"You brought her to see fish? Seriously?"

"I wanted to take her somewhere fun."

"So you took her to see fucking fish swimming around?" Sabien ran his hands through his hair, like I'd told him that his favorite burger joint had finally gotten condemned. "You do understand that we want to impress this woman? What about Chloe suggests that she would like to see your swimmy little friends?"

Crossing my arms, I glared at my brother. "What the hell is your problem? You are literally yelling at me about fish right now!"

"I am not going to let this pack lose our scent match because of your fish-kink."

"It's not a fucking kink."

"Out of the three of us, I thought that you were supposed to be the smart one." Sabien groaned, like he actually thought that me taking Chloe out to the aquarium was the worst thing in the world. I wasn't even going to ask him where he'd take our scent match. Sabien thought that K.N.O.B.B.s burgers were fine dining. "Who the hell made you pack lead?"

Normally, I would remind him that all the guys in the pack did. No one else could be bothered to take the lead. Their exact words were that there was no way in hell that they would put up with all that bureaucratic paperwork nonsense, and now that was my job.

Instead, I grabbed the paper towels off the dispenser and chucked it at his stupid head.

Whatever.

Me and my swimmy little friends hadn't done bad at all, considering I'd ended the date with a kiss. I'd like to see my brother's dumb ass do better.

CHAPTER 15
CHLOE

GOING BACK to my normal routine felt surreal after my date with Kain.

It was like he had pulled me completely out of this world, and shown me a wilder side to life that I'd never even imagined.

Before going on that date, I honestly viewed it as a chore. Kain had weaseled a date out of me, and it was just something that I had to get out of the way. One bad date, that's all I had to tolerate, and then I told myself that I would be free to ditch my scent matches once and for all. The date wasn't meant to go spectacularly well. I wasn't supposed to have so much fun.

My phone vibrated in my pocket.

It was a fight to get it out of my pocket single handedly. My other hand was clutching my food tray and awkwardly trying to balance the drink I'd already placed on it, but I managed it.

Kain: Hey Darling

I wasn't supposed to be smiling down at my phone like an

idiot, but alas. Here I was.

> Kain: Sabien said to wear protective clothing for your date.

Okay?

Well, that was one way to wipe that pesky smile straight off my face.

> Me: What does that even mean?

I stared at the three dots as Kain typed out his answer. How was I just thinking about how glad I was to give my scent matches a chance, *minutes* ago? I hadn't even spoken to Kain's twin and I was already second guessing their pack. Again.

> Kain: Jeans and long sleeves.

> Kain: If my brother annoys you, I will rescue you immediately

It was as if Kain had read my mind. How were these two even brothers?

I frowned at my phone as I picked up my lunch at the cafeteria.

Well I gave one of my scent matches a chance and didn't regret it. Kain and his brother were literally biologically identical. So even though Sabien seemed totally off his rocker, how much would it hurt to give him a chance? It looked like in any case, I was going to have to put up with him if I wanted a relationship with Kain. If he was totally annoying, I would just have to view him as Kain's unfortunate baggage.

Maneuvering my lunch tray to my favorite spot, I sat down at the picnic table with the best view in the entire Institute. I stared down at the food on my tray and buried my face in my palm. Did I really pick up a chocolate and raspberry pie? And nothing else? Food with the exact smell as my scent match… really? I checked my watch. It was still about five minutes until the interview with the next alpha. Maybe I still had time to—

"Are you Chloe Stryker?"

Damn it.

"I heard from Titus that I had to have an interview with you?" The latest alpha was enormous, tall and bulky with a confused look on his handsome face.

Great. Titus sent me another himbo. Well, might as well take advantage of the situation.

"Right. Let's get started. I need to test out your observation and tactical skills." I made sure to enunciate my words and to put a serious look on my face.

"You're sending me on a mission?" The alpha immediately sat up straighter as all traces of confusion were wiped away.

"Yup. I need you to take this tray into the food court. Bring back a turkey sandwich, a fruit cup and a bag of chips. The most important thing is to make sure that no one sees you."

"Got it. Do you need me to bring back the pie, too?" The beefy alpha made a quick attempt to grab it, but instinctively I grabbed the plate, pulling my pie back to safety.

"No, that won't be necessary. Good luck, alpha." I saluted him like I'd seen my dads do, and he actually saluted me back.

I watched as the alpha ran across the outdoor eating area. He braced against the cafeteria door before pulling it wide open and disappearing inside.

For all the nonsense I was putting up with, I definitely deserved a little reward. I scooped up a perfect little bite of chocolatey goodness, making sure to get a little dash of tart raspberry cream, as I typed out a quick message to Titus.

Me: Are you even serious with these alphas? I need to know if you are actually trying to form a decent pack

Titus: What's wrong with Simon?

Titus: Wait...

Titus: Why is Simon army crawling across the cafeteria floor right now?

Me: You're at lunch right now? I thought you had work.

Titus: A friend texted me a picture.

Titus: What did you do?

Me: Wait, what friend?

Me: Is it a guy?

Me: Is he cute?

Titus: You haven't met him

Me: Why?

Me: Is he not hot enough for your pack or something?

Titus: He didn't ask to be in it

I stared at my phone in disbelief.

Titus had guys that he enjoyed spending time with… and instead of thinking to make a pack with men that he actually liked, he was asking me to check out alphas like *Simon?*

Watching Simon sprint back all red-faced, holding on to the lunch tray like his life depended on it, I decided that there was something nice about his single-minded determination, I guess. I mean if that's what you are into, that's fine.

"Alright," Simon was out of breath, with sweat dripping down his face. He was holding up the tray triumphantly. The sandwich looked good, but the fruit cup had fallen over, leaving grapes rolling all around the tray and knocking into the deflated bag of chips. "I tried my best. Think somebody might have seen me at the end, though."

"Excellent work, I'll text Titus with the results." I took the tray from Simon, and finished up texting my brother.

> Me: Titus. If you like this friend

> Me: Then you go ask HIM to join your pack

I jammed my finger down so hard on the send button that my finger actually hurt a tiny bit.

Placing my phone down on the lunch tray, I looked up to see that Simon was still there, watching me.

"Good work alpha. You are dismissed." I nodded to him.

"Thank you for the opportunity Miss Stryker." Simon saluted me again, before turning and finally leaving me alone.

I shook my head as I picked up my hard earned lunch. Technically someone else did the hard-earning, but whatever. I still deserved it.

Well, at least the sandwich was good: juicy turkey with just the right amount of creamy mayo, and a crisp bite of lettuce. Delicious.

My phone lit up once more with a text notification, and I flipped it face down. Unless someone was dying, I was going to eat. Honestly, I'd had enough of alphas for one day.

When it came to love, boys were just dumb sometimes.

CHAPTER 16
SABIEN

WHY DIDN'T Kain warn me that our scent match was hot as fuck?

I felt all the thoughts in my head short-circuiting and going haywire as I looked into our scent match's hazel eyes. She had the kind of eyes that shifted in the light. At first, I thought they were a deep blue with flecks of green. When Chloe stepped out into the sunlight, a second glance revealed that they were light green surrounding sweet honey brown.

She had rich auburn hair that fell past her shoulders in silky waves. I wanted to slip my fingers through her hair to see if it was as soft as it looked, and pull her close enough to kiss her senseless.

Then there was her scent. Pure sugary goodness that reminded me of velvety frosting. A perfect spiral of soft-serve ice cream on a hot day. She was the buttercream in the cake. A burst of sweetness that was exploding across my tongue. High fructose corn syrup surging through my veins.

She was the best of everything.

Decadent. Luxurious.

Vanilla.

Oh. I'd been staring at her like a complete idiot. My bad.

"Sorry for staring. You're fucking gorgeous." I told her.

My blunt statement startled a laugh out of her. The sound of her laughter was high and light, tinkling in the air like a delicate wind chime, and cut through the awkward first date tension. I wasn't expecting her to laugh like that at all, when she first came in with a boss bitch expression on her face.

There was something about her energy that just resonated with me. It was unexpected, considering how she had gotten along so well with my brother, but the vibes between us were just right. "Do you want to check out the best burgers in New Oxford?"

"Burgers sound great. I'm starving." Chloe smiled.

King's burger shack was a hidden gem—a gem in a trash heap. No really, it was one of those places that looked sketchy, rough around the edges, with permanent cobwebs in the corner of the billboards that simply read 'New Oxford's Best Burgers.' They probably should have named it anything else, considering how the exterior looked like a sketchy cockroach hotel. Not enough people gave it a chance, though the burgers here were out of this world.

Chloe ordered the number three with swiss cheese, bacon and avocado because my girl had that refined taste. She wasn't a heathen like me who got the number eight, a burger that was slathered with barbeque sauce on top of old-fashioned cheddar and an onion ring.

She stared at her burger as if she was searching the meat and cheese for traces of poison. Eventually, she took a tentative bite.

"Oh, wow." Her eyes lit up at the taste.

"I know right."

K. N. O. B. B's really did have New Oxford's Best Burgers: juicy meat with a burst of flavors.

"I think that this might be the best burger I've had in my

life." Chloe took a bigger chunk out of her burger, and chewed thoughtfully for a moment. "So this place looks a little rough, but did I really need protective clothing to eat burgers?"

I ducked my head, hiding a smirk. My girl was going to love the plans for the evening, even though she had no idea that she was going to love it. "No, we're just getting started."

The outside of Super Smash could have been any office. The walls were beige-painted brick, with a darker awning. There was nothing that identified it as a rage room. Even the little sign neatly printed on the window just had the store hours under the swirly typography of their trademark.

But just one step inside and it was clear that Super Smash was something different. The squares of protective padding stapled to the wall were a dead giveaway. Or maybe it was the array of weapons, baseball bats, golf clubs, crowbars, and hammers. If all that wasn't clear enough, there was a rack of gear with helmets, goggles and jumpsuits lined up.

Chloe looked around with wide eyes as I stepped up to the front counter.

"Reservation for room four." I pointed to the room that was marked simply by number.

The skinny attendant, with tattoos creeping up to his neck and the employee badge labeled "Ben," nodded. Good ole' Ben typed something onto his computer to confirm our appointment and register our waivers, before directing us over to the display of protective gear.

Chloe and I suited up and approached the weapons.

"Ladies first." I stepped back, letting Chloe get the first crack at choosing her instrument of destruction.

Chloe approached the weapons cautiously, as if she was worried that one of them was going to get mad, come to life and start yelling at her. She trailed her hands a few inches above the various weapons as if afraid to touch them, before hovering over the golf club, and picking it up. She patted the blunt edge against her open palm, testing it.

"Good choice," I winked at her, before strolling over to the metal baseball bat. I grabbed it, tapping it against my knee in anticipation. "You ready, gorgeous?"

Chloe trailed behind me hesitantly as I opened up room four.

In the middle of the room was a car. It was a simple sedan, with the green paint chipping off in some places, but otherwise untouched. Sweet. They must have just refreshed their inventory.

"After you," I gestured to the car with my bat.

"So I can just hit this?" Chloe tapped the car gently with the putter.

I nodded at her encouragingly.

Chloe drew her putter back before smashing it into the car windshield hard, shattering all the glass in a bullseye pattern.

A wide smile spread across my face.

Chloe twirled her putter around in her hands, getting into it. She circled the car like a predator, her eyes lingering on all the parts that looked the most vulnerable. Suddenly she struck again. Her putter crashed into the taillights in an explosion of little bits of red plastic.

There was something fantastically hot about watching my scent match smash the car into smithereens. The way that her eyes narrowed as she swung, the glorious spray of glass and bits of metal exploding in the wake of her fury.

She was magnificent.

Sultry vanilla filled the room. The aroma seemed even sweeter now that it was mixed with the faint scent of car dust, iron and destruction.

Just like I thought, Chloe was filled to the brim with pent up rage.

I'd suspected it ever since Kain had first described her. How her head was always in a book. Always rushing from class to class, pushing herself to the max. My girl was winding herself up way too tightly. Chloe might not know it, but she was nothing but a bundle of tension. Living on the edge of a total mental breakdown. Desperate for release.

Now Chloe was panting, her face flushed and eyes bright. Somehow, she looked even hotter like this, slightly disheveled, and letting it all out. The car was dented all over, with every single piece of glass in tiny shards on the floor.

"Remind me to never make you angry," I muttered.

CHAPTER 17
CHLOE

I COULDN'T SAY why Sabien made me lose control.

He wasn't the kind of guy I ever thought I'd be interested in. If anyone, I always saw myself with someone like Kain. Kain reminded me of myself. He was the responsible one. I was willing to bet cold hard cash that Kain was a straight A student. The kind of guy who kept his room tidy and who would do the dishes without anyone having to ask him to do it.

In comparison, Sabien's energy was wild.

He had that same handsome face that I was already drawn to because of Kain, but being with him could not feel more different. On the outside, he appeared calm and put together. Beneath it, his energy was explosive. He was a whirlwind, a natural disaster. Like he was always on the cusp of some impromptu adventure, or of throwing himself straight into danger.

Being with him felt like flinging off a bra after a long day.

Before spending time with him, I had no idea that he was exactly what I needed. I felt freed from a cage that I didn't even know that I'd fallen into. I felt like I'd been thrown straight into the deep end, into the refreshing waters that soothed away all the stress I didn't even know was there.

It was Sabien's turn. He had been leaning casually against the wall, eyes never leaving me. But now, as he appraised the damage I'd done, I could see the animal hunger in his expression. Something wild within him was rising to the surface, happy to be let out to play.

Suddenly he slammed his bat down, cracking across the hood of the car with the explosive crash of metal on metal.

Damn. He hit *hard.*

Sabien didn't stop there, swinging the bat again and again, until the entire door frame twisted under the force of the blows. Even under the protective suit, I could see how his biceps flexed with each swing, how the muscles in his back bunched up.

Oh, *fuck.*

He was sexy.

I couldn't help it. All the chaos and destruction within him was drawing me in. I was the moth flirting with the flame. Captivated by the disaster. I wouldn't be able to stop myself if I tried.

Sabien abruptly stopped pummeling the car, as his eyes met mine.

It was as if he could read the emotions rioting within me as if they were written all over my face. He dropped his baseball bat, letting it clatter to the floor. Sabien headed over and pulled me close. Wrapping his arms around me until my waist was nestled against his. Until I could feel his hardness pressing against me, impossible to ignore.

I couldn't help it, all I wanted was to feel him closer.

"You want to get out of here?" His smooth voice was a purr in my ear.

Yes. Yes, I wanted that so bad that it shocked me.

CHAPTER 18
CHLOE

LEAVING the rage room was a blur. My stomach was tight with anticipation, and my heart was pounding as I somehow changed and made my way back into Sabien's car.

I held his hand during the drive, and could feel that Sabien's pulse was racing just as hard as mine. Sabien stroked his thumb along my wrist. Heat flooded my lower belly at the feel of his rough hands.

Should I tell him that I'd never done this before?

Something told me that he was barely holding on to control. That he only *looked* calm, but really he was ready to throw me on to a bed and unleash all that wild energy on me. I could feel it bottled up inside of him.

I should probably tell him… but a part of me really didn't want to.

Sabien was looking at me like I was making him lose his mind, and a part of me wanted him completely unrestrained. I wanted him to lose control.

I didn't want my first time to be soft and safe. There was just something about Sabien that made me want to rip all my clothes off and ride him like tomorrow didn't exist.

I barely noticed anything but him as Sabien brought me to

a modern house with large windows smack in the middle of the suburbs. I got vague impressions of an industrial style chandelier and a black leather sofa in front of an electric fireplace with blue flames. Sabien pulled me quickly through the sleek living room and up the stairs, and I was practically running to keep up with him.

Sabien led me into a room, and I got a brief impression of a neatly made bed and a closet that seemed to be bursting at the seams with clothing shoved out of the way… and then he was on me. Sabien pressed me right into the door. His big, strong body pushed me against the wood panels.

Sabien pressed heated, open-mouthed kisses down my neck. With each touch of his hot lips against my skin, sparks of electricity ran down my spine. With each kiss, I was wrapped up deeper and deeper in my need for this man. Every thought clouded in red-hot desire.

Sabien slid his fingertips under the hem of my shirt, tracing a path across my stomach. His touch burned, lighting every inch of my skin on fire.

He made me feel so fucking good.

Sabien grabbed my waist, grinding me against him, until I could feel his hardness, that tantalizing promise of friction right where I needed him. His other hand slid up to my chest, pushing my bra roughly out of the way until he was palming my breasts boldly. He grabbed my nipple, rolling it between his fingers.

I gasped as he tugged at my sensitive peaks, the pressure there echoing deep in my lower belly, flooding my core until I was dripping for him.

Sabien grabbed my hips, lifting me, urging me to wrap my legs around his waist. All I knew was the touch of his lips as he pressed his mouth against mine in a rough kiss. He carried me across the room to his bed, falling with me onto the sheets, pressing his delicious weight over me.

Sabien shoved my shirt up, tugging it off so hard that the

fabric ripped. That would have annoyed me if Sabien hadn't then unclipped my bra with one hand and then bent down to my breast, sucking my nipple and what felt like half of my entire left tit into his mouth.

My back arched off the bed as I gasped.

Fuck.

The intense suction against my sensitive flesh was making me see stars.

He swirled his tongue around my nipple, and the contrast of harsh suction and his tongue's caresses had me squirming. I bucked my hips against his, and Sabien groaned as it brushed against his rock-hard cock.

I had both of my hands beneath his shirt, half feeling the hard ridges of his muscles, half trying to tug his shirt off him. Sabien rose to his knees and pulled off his shirt in one smooth motion.

His hands dropped down to his belt, tugging it off and throwing it across the room. He unzipped his pants, and drew them down slowly, releasing his cock.

My jaw dropped.

Well, *damn.*

Were cocks supposed to be *that* big? His girth was thicker than my wrist. There was no way... they definitely didn't look that enormous in any of my text books.

Sabien tilted his head at me, as if he were silently asking if I still wanted to do this. I unfastened the buttons on my own jeans, tugging them down along with my panties, as if to say, hell yes. He helped me, yanking off the offending fabric, pulling until they were all the way off.

I was totally naked beneath him.

Wait.

He'd left my socks on. That seemed like some kind of fashion crime. Shouldn't we—

Sabien slid the tip of his cock against my entrance and all thoughts of socks died.

His hardness glided across my entrance, pressing right against my clit, right where I needed him.

I moaned, helplessly. Parting my legs wider, pleading with him silently.

It wasn't enough, I needed *more*.

I needed Sabien to give it to me.

Sabien had been watching my face carefully. He seemed to know exactly what I needed, because he reached down and positioned his cock at my entrance.

Warmth pushed between my legs, hard against my walls. Blinding pressure, that was so much, so intense. Veering right on the cusp between pain and pleasure.

My breath shuddered as Sabien thrust in deeper.

The friction was delicious, but intense. There was so much. I felt as if the pressure was splitting me apart.

I must have been wincing, because Sabien stopped moving and reached down. His rough finger found my clit, and started rubbing tantalizing circles. With just the perfect pressure, right where I needed it.

Sabien pressed his lips to my throat and began to suck. Hard. Biting the skin right in the spot where the bond would go.

The smooth pressure against my clit. His mouth, hard against my throat. Teeth against my skin. That hint of his claim on me... all of it was so much, building something inside of me. Something that was teetering between rough pleasure and sweet pain, making me lose the last bit of my control.

I dug my nails into his back as an orgasm ricocheted through me.

Waves pulsed through my core, rippling down my entire body. I was sinking. Drowning in pleasure. Completely weighed down by it.

Sabien kissed me through my orgasm, rocking his hips in sensuous motions, helping me ride out the waves of bliss.

Coming down from the high, I felt like every inch of me went loose, like Sabien had churned my body into melty butter. Like I had been transformed into a happy goo.

Then Sabien started to move.

Sabien thrust his cock into me hard. So deep inside of me I could feel him in my stomach. I could feel every inch of him inside of me, every ridge of that fat cock as he fucked me. Pulling almost all of the way out, only to slam back into me. Brutally fast.

I moaned.

It was all so much. The delicious friction, the hot feel of his cock against my walls. Each time he drove his cock into me, I became more lost in it. He took me with wild, ferocious thrusts. I spread my legs wider to welcome each one.

His movements became faster. Frantic. As if he was chasing something that he could only find within me. As if he were nothing but a rutting beast. As if he were a sinner trying to exorcize his demons between my thighs.

With a deep groan, he drove his cock into me completely, until his hips were grinding against me. Erasing any space between us until I couldn't tell where he stopped and I began.

I could feel him pulsing inside of me. I could feel the heat of his cum as his cock throbbed deep inside me.

Then I felt the base of his cock swelling thick. His knot grew fat, squeezing even tighter against my inner walls. Stuffing me to the brim, almost to the point of pain. Connecting us even tighter.

Okay.

I'd just lost my virginity in a wild uncontrolled frenzy.

Me. I did that.

I didn't even recognize myself. But somehow, I liked this new version of me, stuffed tight and satisfied on a fat alpha knot.

CHAPTER 19
SABIEN

SEX WITH CHLOE was mind blowing. Absolutely out of this world. My body was humming with bliss, like a shot of distilled euphoria pumping through my veins. All the noise and chaos in my head quieted to sweet pleasure. More than anything, I was sated and ready to take a nap.

But Chloe was not on the same page. I had flipped her so that she was laying on top of me, but my sweet princess was starting to get fidgety. Chloe wiggled her hips, tugging on my knot. I don't know what she was trying to do, but what ended up happening was that the added friction triggered another burst of cum to flood into her.

"Wait, so we are just stuck here?" Chloe didn't look like she was upset or anything, but then again she didn't look happy to find out that even though we were done with sex, we weren't really done having sex.

"Is this your first time taking a knot?" I really should have asked her that kind of thing before sex… but it's like a delicate balance. I didn't want to fuck up the mood by asking twenty million questions when she was giving me the green light.

"This was my first time having sex, like ever. I was a virgin at the start of our date."

Oh shit.

Why hadn't I noticed that our omega was a virgin? Her first time should have been at a five star heat hotel—the ones with the lux edition omega nests, sheets made of Egyptian cotton, and enough pillows to smother a baby elephant.

Instead, her first time was in my room... which in my defense, I had cleaned. A little. Not that I was sure that sex was going to happen tonight, but at least I had remembered to make my bed with clean sheets. Just in case.

"Well, you got to wait until I... uh, go down..." Now did not seem like a good time to bring up how long it usually took for my knot to completely deflate. Nor the fact that I could tell from how stiff the base was that it was going to take longer than usual.

"But I've got a paper to finish." Chloe had twisted her head around to get a look at the alarm clock on my dresser.

Well, *ouch.*

"Doesn't this feel good to you?" I was literally still inside of her, harder than I'd ever been in my life. My cock was swollen against her luscious walls. Did she really want to do a paper over doing *me*? I guess that wasn't a fair thought, as she had already done me. I guess not everyone is an after-knot snuggler.

"Well, yeah, it's amazing, but I got deadlines."

"Do you want me to call someone to go get your paper?" I'd give Kain a ring. He said that he'd be going out with Brutus. Kain would give me an earful about sleeping with our scent match on the first date. But then again, honestly, when did my brother *not* give me an earful?

"Could you do that for me?" Chloe had the sweetest expression on her face, like I was a hero for doing this for her. How could I say no to that?

I reached down to my jeans that were just within reach,

digging around in the pockets until I found my phone. I clicked on the top number in my contacts and called.

"Hello?" a gruff voice answered.

Oh shit. It was not my brother who picked up the call.

"Uhh," I couldn't not say it. Though she was half-dazed and sleepy, Chloe was still watching me. I scrambled to come up with a way to get the words out that would result in Brutus not wanting to tear me a new one... but came up with nothing. "Is Kain around?"

"What did you do?" Brutus' enunciated each word harshly, as if he had caught me doing something wrong.

I could feel him through the part of the bond I hadn't managed to shut out. Brutus was getting pissed at me, big time... which wasn't even fair. I hadn't even said anything to him. This was just lingering bitterness over the whole sandwich incident.

I had no choice now but to say it.

"I'm with Chloe, she wanted to know if someone could pick up her essay."

"And why can't you get it?" Brutus challenged me.

"I can't move. I'm knotted in her." As soon as I said it, I winced as Brutus' anger grew to a fever pitch in the bond.

"You've got to be fucking with me. There's no way that you're being serious right now." His voice somehow got even lower.

"I'm sorry, but she said she has a deadline..."

"What the hell? How did you fuck up the fucking? If you'd done her right that essay would be the last thing on her mind." If Brutus was here right now, I could picture him snapping his belt as he prepared to discipline me.

Damn it, why did that make me even harder? That was not helping anything. I had to get it through to my other head currently controlling me (the smaller one, that isn't just a dick but is also being a dick) that we were currently mad at Brutus. Now was not the time to get aroused by him.

"If I get back home to see our scent match doing home-work while you're inside of her, you'll give me no choice," Brutus went completely calm. Every hair on my arm stood on end, and a jolt went up my spine, spreading warmth all the way through me, and making my cock twitch in anticipation. "I am going to have to teach you what a good fuck looks like. I'll teach you until you can't fucking *walk* for a week."

"Got it. No essay needed, sir." I hung up the phone in a hurry. Letting it drop to the ground.

Chloe raised an eyebrow at me. "Something tells me we're going to be here for a while."

"Sorry," I took a deep breath, trying to still the racing beat of my heart. "He's, uhh, unavailable at the moment."

CHAPTER 20
BRUTUS

I'D HAD my eye on the twins immediately.

The moment I saw them, I knew in my gut that the two of them were everything I'd ever wanted for a pack. What wasn't obvious was why none of the others had realized it. But that didn't matter now.

They were mine.

I'd come in and snatched them up before any other alphas could even wrap their minds around the fact that the two of them weren't even an option anymore. All that was left for the three of us to complete our pack was an omega, perfectly suited to us.

I'd put aside money—for months—working longer hours and cutting back on basic luxuries. Through it all, I kept reminding myself that it would be worth it. They deserved nothing but the best. I was making these sacrifices so that my pack would get the best scent match that the Valentine's Division had to offer.

People often said that the best things in life came free—obviously none of those people had tried caviar.

Then when I was a couple weeks away from putting our deposit down at the Institute, Kain returned home with a dazed look on his face, announcing that he'd found our scent match.

It didn't seem real.

From everything that I'd heard about the statistics and probability, at the bare minimum, it should have taken us *years* after forming our pack to find her.

So I did the only reasonable thing I could—I paid a hacker to background check Chloe.

Was this omega even who she said she was?

What were the chances that she was actually the sister of an alpha Kain had a crush on? (I'd agreed with Kain about interviewing for Titus' pack, because obviously I'd do anything to keep my twins happy. Even if it meant sharing them. I could share them... a little. It wasn't as if I was a completely possessive asshole.)

But I'd made a gross error. In waiting to see if Chloe was actually our scent match, and not some woman who'd purchased sketchy pheromones to trap the twins, Sabien had gone and been a little shit.

It had been the first time he'd called me in *weeks*, and I'd found out that he was having bad sex with our scent match.

What the fuck was his problem? He actually thought that it was okay that he'd *bored* her during sex. How was he not ashamed that the little omega actually wanted someone to bring her books to entertain her—when he was still inside of her?

Sabien was on track to fuck up the entire pack's chances with our scent match before I even had a chance to meet her.

Besides, the background check revealed that she was who she said. Her family just had like a few dozen kids. It only made sense that our scent match was related to that guy Kain had been drooling all over.

The report also revealed that Chloe was on track to becoming the Valedictorian of her class. Her academic perfor-mance was pristine—she'd never even gotten less than a ninety-seven on any of her exams. It was at that moment that I knew that I had made a mistake. Obviously this girl was our scent match—I'd always known that our omega would be phenomenal.

All I had to do was unfuck up the mess Sabien had left for me.

I'd let him get away with too much recently—he'd pissed me off so bad that I had taken to avoiding him, rather than correcting all of his misbehavior.

It was just about time for me to fuck the attitude out of him.

CHAPTER 21
CHLOE

SO, I imagined that I wasn't the kind of person who would sleep with a guy on the first date. Considering the fact that I had gone on just a first date, and I'd slept with Sabien, I guess I was learning new things about myself.

I also hadn't anticipated how I would behave in the aftermath of getting laid—I launched myself headfirst into my studies. Was I academically motivated before? Yes. Yes, I was. But now? I was cranking out essays like my life depended on it. I didn't even know I had more ass to bust, until I was busting my ass even more.

Ever since our date, Kain had gotten into the habit of joining me for dinners. He'd make small talk with me, as I frantically did homework. Sabien joined as well, though he didn't talk so much as he dramatically leaned on things and played with his phone. Grunting in agreement occasionally as Kain tried to force him to join in on the conversation.

All of my academic overload had led to this—I had a night free. I was actually ahead enough that I could spend some time with my new favorite alphas.

"So I'm actually a little ahead of all my assignments." I brushed a strand of hair behind my ear, trying to look casual.

Kain gave me a thumbs up and a smile. A silent good job.

Somehow, Sabien knew exactly what I was getting at. He looked at me sharply like a dog who just noticed a chunk of steak had fallen to the floor.

"Do you have any idea of who you want to do with all of your spare time?" Sabien asked me straight out.

Kain's jaw dropped. He looked like he was frantically formulating an apology on his brother's behalf.

"Do I have to choose?" I looked from one brother to another. I let a tiny bit of hunger into my expression, as I bit my lip.

I swear, I wasn't this kind of girl. I was a freaking virgin, like a week or so ago. But Sabien had unlocked this horny beast that I didn't know was inside of me.

That beast wanted to come out to play.

Sabien scooped me straight out of my chair and carried me off in front of everyone. It would have been totally embarrassing, if the dining room hadn't been half empty.

"Come on, bro. Get with the program." Sabien snapped at his brother, who was watching all of this unfold as if he was trying and failing to connect all the dots in his head. "Grab the keys and start the car. We've got an omega to satisfy."

CHAPTER 22
CHLOE

I HAD GOTTEN USED to the twins. Together they were confident and easygoing, with an energy that I just clicked with. But the two of them were nothing that I couldn't handle.

Everything felt different once the shirts came off.

I bit my lip at the pair of abs in front of me. Sabien and Kain were blonde and blue-eyed perfection. Golden twins that looked like they were meant to be laying sprawled out on a litter, while fanned by giant palm fronds. And the two of them turned all of the heat of that delicious perfection on me.

Did I really want to do this?

The twins were watching me with matching expressions, eyes-half lidded with lust, and a hunger so fierce that it *burned.*

Yes. Definitely yes.

I swallowed, deciding to lay it all out. It didn't make sense for me to give the two of them any false expectations before we could even get properly started. I wouldn't want anyone getting hurt over all of this.

"Do I need to like suck one of you off while the other is fucking me? To be perfectly honest, I am not that coordinated.

I worry that I might like… bend it the wrong way. Just thinking about it will make me like… not be able to get off."

The twins glanced at each other, communicating something without words. Sabien lifted one eyebrow, and Kain shrugged, before reassuring me out loud.

"We are literally brothers. I can wait my turn if that is what you want."

"Yeah, make Kain wait. Besides, this is not a porno. You don't have to worry about doing things wrong or right. The important thing is what feels right for you. What you are ready for."

"Don't worry about us." Kain was suddenly close. So close, until the sharp lines of his jaw, the masculine appeal of his handsome face. He was right there, cupping my face in his big hand, brushing one rugged finger against my lower lip. He leaned down and pressed a soft kiss to my lips.

The lush, decadent scent of chocolate was everywhere, pressing into me, sinking straight into my pores.

"We're going to take care of you," Sabien murmured into my skin, as he pressed hot open mouthed kisses along my neck and across my shoulder. He brushed his hand under my shirt, leaving a trail of fire on each inch of skin that he touched. His soft caresses stirred something in me, lighting each of my nerve endings on fire. Igniting a heat that echoed down deep within my core.

Sabien's sweet scent, a primal burst of ripe strawberries was added into the mix. I tried very hard not to think about the fact that the three of us together must smell just like Neapolitan ice cream.

My worries started to fade away around the same time the twins' pants vanished.

I'd wondered if the two of them would be identical *everywhere.*

Considering Sabien had the biggest dick I'd ever seen, I'd been curious about Kain's too.

Alright, so it wasn't like I had all the alphas in the world dropping their pants in front of me and letting me check them with a tape measure. But I did have eight brothers. Too many of them had awful habits when it came to laundry… suddenly realizing that their last remaining underwear was also dirty. That was just to say that these weren't the first pair of dicks I'd seen.

But they certainly were the biggest.

In a motion so smooth, I barely even felt it, Sabien drew my shirt over my head and tossed it into a corner of the room. With a subtle twitch of his fingers, he unclasped my bra. Slowly, he drew the straps down my shoulders, letting my bra fall to the floor.

I leaned back into Sabien as his kisses grew more heated. He wrapped his arms around me, cupping my breasts and pinching my nipples until I was gasping and arching back into him.

In front of me, Kain had dropped to his knees, staring at me like I was the most delicious thing on the menu.

What was he doing?

Kain popped open the button of my jeans and drew the zipper down. Slowly, like he was opening up a present, Kain pulled my jeans and panties down my legs. A shiver went down my spine as I realized that for the first time, I was completely bare in front of him.

Kain leaned in closer, until he was right in-between my thighs. Gazing at my pussy like it was a renaissance painting. With such reverence that it was starting to make me squirm.

Then Kain pressed his hot tongue right against my pussy, stroking between my folds as if he wanted to *consume* me.

I shrieked.

Bucking my hips right into his face, I lost control. I hadn't expected anything to feel so *intense.*

Kain grabbed both of my thighs and looked up at me, with a questioning gaze.

"No one's ever done that before," I told him after I managed to catch my breath.

Kain looked up sharply at his brother, giving him the dirtiest look I'd ever seen on that handsome face. I could feel Sabien shuffle awkwardly behind me.

What? Was this something that I should expect from the alphas I slept with?

Even though I had literally spent months learning about sexuality in my classes, I felt so unprepared. So out of my depth.

The thoughts rolled straight out of my head as Kain pressed his mouth to my pussy once more. His tongue searched out my clit, and once he found that delicate nub, he caressed it. Stroked it with tantalizing pressure, then pressed his lips right over my clit and sucked.

The friction was so intense, I lost it. My head fell back onto Sabien's shoulder as all the pleasurable sensations took over.

I was drowning. Lost in each lusty swipe of his tongue. Held in place by Kain's strong grip on my thighs, and Sabien's arms around my chest. If the two of them weren't holding me, I would have melted completely away. I needed them—both of them—to ground me. As the pleasure built and built... until I felt like I lost myself entirely.

My orgasm ripped through me in pulsing waves. So intense that my legs began to shake. I would have slipped down to the floor if Kain wasn't bracing me with his strong arms. He kept his lips on me, helping me ride out the intense pleasure, making love to me with his tongue.

Sabien scooped me up and placed me in the middle of the bed, as Kain lay next to me.

Kain leaned in to whisper in my ear, "I'm here for you. You can tell me what you need. Exactly what you need."

His deep voice against my ear made my pussy clench up with want. Clenching on nothing. This man was so damn sexy. I needed him. Needed *more*.

Kain tilted my face towards him as he kissed me. *This* wasn't like the tender kisses we had shared before. He was rougher. Hungrier. As he deepened the kiss, I could taste myself, sweet and musky on his tongue.

Warmth pooled in my lower belly.

The twins had me so wet, I could feel myself dripping down my thighs.

I needed them. Needed them *bad.*

Desire was circling through my brain, so heavily that I was dizzy with it.

I squirmed helplessly, against this overwhelming ache within me. An ache that was pounding through my veins, making me crazy. Making me desperate for them.

Breaking away from Kain's lips, I moaned, "please."

"Please what, darling?" Kain trailed his fingers down my lower belly, halting away from where I needed him. Teasing me with that tantalizing promise of friction. "Tell me what you need."

Damn him for making me say it. Kain was going to literally drive me crazy.

"I need more." My breaths were getting jagged. I tried to buck my hips, seeking out the sweet friction that was the only thing that could soothe this insanity churning through me.

"More?" Kain was suddenly brushing his fingers down my pussy, stroking delicate patterns against my clit.

I grabbed his hand, pushing him more firmly between my thighs. I held his hand there like he was an anchor, like every-thing would be lost without those confident strokes brushing me, right *there,* in my core, where I was somehow both burning and drenched for him.

Kain eased a finger inside of me, then thrust it within me, deep.

My walls gripped him each time he pulled too far out of me, needing the soothing friction… needing him.

Kain pressed another finger into me and started to fuck

me with them. Fast and rough. In a steady pattern, that made my breath hitch. That was building pleasure within me... so blindingly fast and intense that it was too much. Too soon...

I started to whine, high-pitched and desperate. In a voice that didn't sound anything like me, but was more honest than any other noise I had made in my entire life.

Kain leaned close to whisper, "Darling, this pleasure is all for you. You can take it. You can take all we have to give you."

His praise crystallized in my mind, then shattered me.

I moaned as I came, white-knuckling the bed sheets, my face flushed. Desire pounded through me.

Holy fuck.

Why did that feel so much more intense the second time?

Kain kissed me as I came down from my high, just a sweet brush of his mouth against mine. He was watching me with a smirk, like he knew that he'd absolutely rocked my entire world.

I mean, it was true. He had.

Sabien was kneeling between my legs, he gripped my thighs and pushed them further apart. He was staring at my pussy with a heat so intense that it made my breath hitch. Even after two orgasms, he had my clit throbbing with need, just with his gaze.

I wrapped my arms around his neck and pulled him close. Sabien grabbed the back of my neck, kissing me roughly. Pressing the weight of his body over mine, pushing me into the bed.

He slid his cock against my entrance, making me whimper, helplessly. I clutched him tighter, digging my nails into his back. I needed him so much closer.

Sabien lined his cock up and thrust inside of me. Deep. I was so wet for him that he slid his entire length inside of me, all in one powerful thrust.

Immediately, I canted my hips, taking him deeper.

My nails dug straight into his skin as I clawed at him, desperate for something to hold on to. Sabien pounded into me, with rough, brutal strokes.

I was drowning in bliss. In the sweet friction. In that perfect slide of his fat cock. In the look in his eyes as he took me, his gaze was locked on me, like he would never be able to look away, like he was lost in me.

"You have no idea how perfect you look right now. You're a goddess." Kain's eyes darted to my face, the heat rising up my chest, the way that my back arched, how my hips moved in sync with his brother's thrusts. "Perfect. You take us so well." His voice was like another touch on my body, intensifying everything—all the friction, the delicious feel of his twin's cock moving furiously within me. I don't know how, but his praise just made everything so much... more.

I reached out and grasped Kain's hand and gripped it tightly. Kain squeezed my hand back, letting me know that he was here for me. He was the anchor I needed, as his twin slammed into me, in a ruthless and primal dance. I clutched at his hand in a white knuckled grip, holding on to him desperately. But he never complained, instead Kain watched. His own breath started getting heavier as he leaned in closer to me.

God, he was so handsome—staring at me like he was starving. As if he knew that I was going to be served next, and he was drooling for me.

Sabien gritted his teeth. His biceps flexed as he once again picked up the pace, rutting into me faster now. So fast that I couldn't keep up. He was a force of nature. Thrusting into me so fast, it was like fucking a storm. His heavy balls slapped into my ass each time he dove into me.

He was a beast.

Feral and untamed, unleashing all his ferocity into my body. As if with each sharp thrust he was binding us closer. I felt it more and more. With each thrust, he was claiming me.

Sabien groaned, so deep that I could feel the vibration of it shiver across my skin. He dove inside of me, pulling out enough that I could feel the swell of his knot rubbing against my clit, like a caress.

That was all the warning I got before he came.

He pumped me full of his cum, flooding me with it in a warm rush.

I could feel him throbbing. His knot was thick and pulsing, resting just outside of my pussy.

I had no idea what he was doing to me, how he turned me into this person, but I wanted it. I wanted every drop of that cum inside of me. My body craved it like he was injecting me with a pure jolt of serotonin.

Sabien kissed me roughly, plunging his tongue into my mouth. Feverishly, like he never wanted to stop.

Kain muttered something under his breath that sounded a bit like, didn't even make her come.

No, not this time. But Sabien had certainly done a number on me.

Anyway, I'd already had two orgasms. I thought another one would make me melt straight into the bed.

Sabien pressed another sweet kiss to the top of my forehead, and then gently withdrew, rolling off to the side.

The second he was off of me, Kain wrapped a hand around my hip and pulled me closer to him, until the entire length of my body was pressed against the entire length of his. His scent hung in the air, heavy and luxurious. He was velvety chocolate, and I was getting drunk on the rich aroma. So decadent and sweet. I couldn't wait to get a taste of him.

He was so warm, and being pressed against all those firm muscles was driving me out of my mind. Reawakening the hunger that I would have thought that I had already satisfied.

What were the twins doing to me? It felt like somehow, the rational side of me had been hijacked by some sex-crazed hormonal monster. I couldn't recognize myself. I couldn't get enough.

Kain brushed his fingertips in slow trails across my body. Tracing along the curve of my hips and up my sides.

His touch lit a fire within me. He was burning me, ravaging through every ounce of calm. Igniting me and waking me up. He felt so fucking good, and I didn't under-stand it at all.

"Your skin is like silk. You have no idea how good it feels to touch you." Kain pressed a hot open-mouthed kiss to my neck, right where omegas took the bond. He bit down lightly, not breaking the skin, and *sucked.*

It was as if he had taken more than just a little bit of skin into his mouth, but had managed to suck all of my senses out with it.

Fuck.

A shudder ran down the whole length of my spine when I felt the hard edge of teeth—not biting down, but teasing me. Just a sharp little reminder of more. Of what could be if I let the twins claim me... if I decided that both of them would be mine.

It was as if every drop of blood in my body rushed down from my head, limbs, and every square inch of my body, and flooded into my pussy—which was now overflowing with heat and desire... empty and desperate for the alpha at my side.

It wasn't enough. I needed more of him. I couldn't just sit here. I had to have him inside of me.

I wrapped my leg around his waist, and grinded against him, moving my hips in sensual patterns. "Kain." My voice was pleading. I could feel his hard cock straining against my thigh, and I didn't want to wait anymore. "I need you."

Kain didn't make me ask twice. He reached down and guided himself to my entrance. I felt him prodding me, before sliding inside me with a single deep thrust.

"Fuck," Kain groaned, like I was killing him. "You're so fucking perfect."

He began to move.

While sex with Sabien was wild, making me lose all grip on my control and breaking my sanity into pieces, Kain moved in me like a well choreographed dancer. His thrusts were fluid, with a rhythm that was steady and confident. Though it was his first time with me, he knew exactly how to move to make every inch of my body coil up with anticipation. He knew how to bring me right to the edge.

Kain grabbed my legs, pulling them over his shoulders. He slowed down his thrusts, hitting me harder with each powerful stroke.

I whimpered. I couldn't help it. I was losing myself to this onslaught of pleasure.

Kain's blue eyes stayed fixed on me. He made me feel like I was the most beautiful woman he'd ever seen. All the force of his desire hit me, while he gazed into my eyes, and I was burning with it.

I gripped with my walls, clenching down on his cock. Holding tight. Wanting to keep him inside of me.

Without warning, a third orgasm rocketed through me. It was an explosion in my core, shattering me. Smashing into pieces every part of who I thought I was until there was nothing left. I was nothing but the pleasure singing through my veins, flooding across every inch of my body.

"That's it, darling." Kain groaned.

He ground against me, circling with his hips. Abandoning his measured rhythm entirely to kiss me. Passionately. Capturing my lips with his. He lay his chest against mine, until I could feel every sculpted ridge of his chest. Every inch of him was hard and pressing flush against me.

He drove into me faster now. As if he'd been chasing after something for his entire life, and he'd finally found it in me.

Pounding hard, so hard that I was beginning to find that same thing in him too.

Kain slammed into me deep, then his whole body shuddered. His knot swelled, pressing thick against my pussy walls, filling me and stuffing me to the brink. I could feel his cock pulsing, and the hot liquid of his cum flooding me.

As I lay there, locked into place by my scent match's knot, it hit me—I was falling for him.

Something deep within me came alive, under his touch, his kisses.

This was so dumb. I barely even knew Kain. I knew Sabien even less… But something in me recoiled at the thought of letting them go. The thought of having to give him up made the inside of my stomach shrivel up. Like I was filled with lead and sinking. Like panic was biting through my skull, tearing me apart from the inside.

Whatever the rest of my goals, I wanted to keep Kain… and his brother, too.

Fuck… was I falling in love?

CHAPTER 23
CHLOE

"CRAP." Sabien sat upright from where he had been sprawled comfortably, leaning on the picnic table, and lazily stealing fries from my lunch tray.

"What?" I eyed my tray to see if he had polished off all my fries. But there were still some there. That wasn't the problem.

"Birth control. We never talked about it." He stared at me seriously, like he had literally just thought about it. As if I hadn't had an entire series of lectures dedicated to the subject and was only now considering my reproductive health.

"Oh. That. Yeah, I got an implant."

Sabien must have noticed something about the way I said it. He heard the undertone of scorn, that I hadn't voiced out loud. Like obviously I was on birth control. Did he think I was going to put my secretarial dreams at risk?

"You don't want kids?"

Kids? I might want them. In seven years. Which was a nice number that was more than five (which was too close) and not as far off into the future as ten. Ten years was just too weird to think about.

"It's not that," I sighed. "No, I have like fifteen siblings.

And both my moms are pregnant again. The two of them are on a mission to repopulate the next generation of alphas like all on their own."

"Why?" Sabien asked, popping another fry into his mouth.

Here we go. We had barely had a couple of dates and already I was dragging Sabien into my families' weirdness.

"Well, they have this theory." I didn't know if this theory was the real reason why they kept having kids.

Unbidden, my conversation with Zane popped back into my head. How my moms just had a breeding kink. I did *not* want to think about that.

Wait…

Were kinks genetic? Did that mean that at some point… I might…

Nope. Nope, nope, nope.

I was not going to have my thoughts go there. I'd just tell the polished and sanitized story that my moms told me. "Like all the high-profile packs out there, they have the same combination. There's always one alpha who is a multi-millionaire. One of them is a psycho. Throw in a couple of pretty boys. Mix them all together and they will inevitably end up with a gold-pack omega and swear off children."

"That can't be true. People would start to notice if that was happening." Sabien shook his head.

"No, it is totally true. Take the Kingsmen pack. Three alphas: a pretty boy, an alpha a few sandwiches short of a picnic, and a millionaire." They ended up with Shatter—who was undoubtedly gorgeous and undoubtedly a gold-pack omega. I'd read it all in 'Spill the Tea,' a New Oxford gossip magazine that tracked rich alphas.

"That's just one pack. That doesn't prove anything." Sabien grabbed another fry. I was getting into the conversation now and stopped keeping track of how many he'd stolen from me. Whatever. Some things were more important than French fries.

"There's the Crimson Fury pack." They were super high-profile and had shocked all the tabloids when their sweetheart beta, Vex, ended up being another gold-pack omega.

"Aren't they actors? So they're all rich. Doesn't feel like it should count."

"Yeah, but you got that same formula. Millionaires with a gold-pack."

"But it's not like one of them is a psychopath or something. They are all in the public eye. Someone would have noticed that." Sabien said, waving a French fry emphatically to help prove his point.

"Okay, so maybe that one doesn't count. But then there's the Saint pack. They are a bunch of rich pretty-boys who got with a gold-pack." I reached into my tray for a fry. After making that excellent point, I felt like I deserved a salty little reward. My hand came up empty.

Damn.

"Nope. Not the Saint pack. There is definitely no psycho there."

"Not true." I lowered my voice, really getting into the conspiracies now. "I heard that the original lead in that pack was a psycho."

"Oh, that's why Havoc killed her alpha?"

"Exactly."

CHAPTER 24
CHLOE

I WAS SMILING and acting like everything was fine, but inside my mind was racing.

This was Stupid Lunch Interview for alpha number twenty-one, Nyle, and I was running into some serious problems. This was more problematic than realizing that the alpha I was interviewing was my scent match—and THAT had been a major hiccup to all of my carefully planned and diagramed life ambitions.

Nyle had dreamy green eyes and windswept brown hair, with that boy-next door charm. Though he was not my type, (right now I'd developed a taste for hot blonde and blue eyed twins) Nyle was drop dead gorgeous, and not doing anything obviously offensive. Since this was one of Titus' pack candidates, there had to be something wrong with him. There had been something off or wrong with *every* single alpha Titus had sent my way so far. My work was cut out for me to figure out just what was wrong with *this* one.

It was time for me to dust off my Red Flag Alpha Asshole Checklist.

Nyle hadn't done anything obviously rude.

He hadn't come to the lunch interview late. Hadn't said

anything misogynistic. He hadn't even talked too much about himself or challenged me why I thought I had the necessary skill to even bother interviewing him at all—that had been the mistake of alpha number nine—which was great. I was able to cancel interview nine super early and use all that extra time for some much-needed studying.

Alright, he'd passed the first test. But that didn't mean that Nyle wasn't hiding the fact that he was a raging, emotionally disturbed monster.

It was time to move on to the second test on my Asshole Checklist—did he have anger issues? I typically found that the easiest way to trigger anger issues in alphas was simply to ignore them. Any alpha with a chip on his shoulder, or an over-inflated sense of his own importance, tended to lose his mind once the spotlight wasn't shining directly on him. Some alphas needed to constantly be drowning in attention, or they'd snap just like a little yappy dog who'd gotten his bone stolen from him.

"So, would you say that you're enjoying your classes at the Institute?" Nyle asked me politely, just continuing the conversation. He had no idea that the jig was about to be up.

"Yeah, hold on." I pulled out my phone and clicked straight to the contacts.

Me: Hey

Kain: Hey yourself, Gorgeous

Me: So why are we not talking about Brutus?

A bubble with three lines popped up on the bottom of my screen and then disappeared.

The fact that there was a whole alpha in their pack that I'd never seen was… honestly kind of weird. I'd gone to their pack house multiple times, and I'd never even spoken to him.

Hell, I'd slept with most of my scent matches and then there was one that I hadn't even spoken to. I didn't even know what he looked like. It was almost like they were hiding him.

> Me: Is Brutus a cannibal serial killer or something?

Out of the corner of my eyes, I was tracking Nyle, to see if he was starting to get agitated with the silent treatment—but no. Nyle was using the lull in the conversation to patiently eat his sandwich. He looked ready to wait for me to finish what I was doing, without interrupting me even a little.

Okay. Either he was even more malicious than any other alpha I'd interviewed before, masking the depths of his depravity and evil... or he was potentially a nice guy. I grit my teeth. If this guy was an asshole, I'd find out soon enough. There was no hiding from my red flag checklist.

> Kain: Brutus is hot enough to be a maneater, but he's not a cannibal

Apparently, Kain thought that wasn't an appropriate reply, as the next two texts came in rapid fire.

> Kain: We didn't want to overwhelm you with all of us at once.

> Kain: He's looking forward to meeting you.

Hot enough to be a man eater? Was that supposed to be a compliment? Wait. What exactly was a man eater? Was it some kind of sexual thing about eating men? Whatever. It wasn't in the Institute approved curriculum, so it couldn't be all that important.

> Me: Is he free this weekend?

> Kain: Hold on, I'll go ask him

Out of the corner of my eye, I could tell that Nyle was getting a bit fidgety. He was almost finished with his sandwich.

If he was going to get pissy with me, he would have done it already.

Fine.

I'd tentatively cross anger issues off the red flag checklist.

What was the next thing on my list? Oh yes. I'd see if Nyle could respect personal boundaries. I'd give him a weird one and see if he would feel tempted to violate it.

"I don't feel comfortable eating when someone else's tray is too close. Would you mind giving me a little bit of space?"

Nyle raised an eyebrow, and shifted his tray back an inch. He didn't say a word about how there was already over a foot between our lunch trays.

"Thank you," I had a demure smile on my face.

Damn it.

Thought I would get him with that one. Okay, so obviously Nyle didn't have problems with respecting boundaries. But he had to have something wrong with him. There was no way that Titus managed to find someone this attractive, with not a single red flag to speak of. It was mathematically impossible.

Alright, I had time during this interview for one more test. It was time to check if Nyle was a covert sociopath, or at very least a narcissist.

"All my classes are really cutting into my time for hobbies. I haven't been able to read anything for fun in weeks." I had googled enough about mirroring to know that everyone did it to an extent. But no one did it with the same intensity as a sociopath—all to create intense feelings of connection in their victim, just to manipulate them.

"Oh, you like reading? What books do you like to read?" Nyle asked me politely.

"The last book I got to read was a romance with a were-wolf pirate, and his adventures in getting *all* of the booty. What about you? What books do you like to read?"

Here was the moment of truth. Was Nyles going to fake an interest in a one-eyed, peg legged swashbuckling wolf? Sorry, but if he even tried it, it was going to be obvious as hell.

"Well, reading isn't my thing. But I do pick up Self Improvement books. It is fascinating to learn from the greats about different tips on improving oneself."

"Oh." I said politely.

Nyle was making zero attempt to mirror me.

It was almost like all of his strong endeavors to hide his dark past were working so effectively, because he wasn't actually hiding anything. Nyle was just a nice guy (not one of those nice guys who just pretend to be nice, to sleaze their way into someone's pants, and if he doesn't get there reveals himself as a raging incel. I mean, actually kind). A nice guy who was built enough to wrestle a bear, with a perfectly symmetrical face.

Huh.

I somehow found an alpha that I could genuinely recommend to Titus for his pack.

Oh right, I should probably show some interest in the thing that he just said—though the thought of reading a Self Improvement book sounded about as fun as stepping on a lego in the middle of the night. "What was the best bit of advice from the books?"

"Probably that," Nyle tapped his index finger against his chin, "I get to choose which of my thoughts I pay attention to. That a negative thought I have about myself is only powerful if I pay attention to it."

Okay, so this guy literally spoke 'therapy' as if it was a

second language to him. That was about as opposite to a sociopathic cannibal serial killer as an alpha could get.

"Well, that's all the time I have for this interview. I'll text Titus the results in one to two business days." I drummed my fingers against the table.

Nyle nodded, holding his hand out to me. He shook my hand with a nice firm grip, without doing that asshole thing that some guys do, where they crush your hand a little bit to show how tough they are.

No. Nyle didn't even crush my hand a little. Just gripped my hand firmly, shaking it with confidence before he continued on his way.

Ugh. Fine. Not only was there nothing wrong with him, Nyle seemed obnoxiously perfect. He and my brother could walk off into the sunset together and have an emotionally mature, boundary respecting and healthy relationship together.

My phone buzzed, so I flipped it back over.

Kain: You have a date with Brutus. Saturday at 3 pm at our packhouse.

CHAPTER 25
CHLOE

I'M NOT GONNA LIE. This Brutus situation had me more than a little concerned.

Here I was, monitoring red flags for my brother, and then walking willy nilly into what could potentially be a date with a giant red flag hidden amongst my own scent matches.

Why hadn't the twins mentioned anything about Brutus before? Why was he this big giant secret? Was this a normal thing? If someone in the pack ended up being a little bit weird, was it a common practice for other members of the pack to sort of lock him away in dark rooms and in chains, and pretend like everything was fine?

Neither of the twins acted like it was weird at all that Brutus hadn't reached out to me himself, and that he was using Kain as a middle man. They both acted like it was also fine that Brutus expected me to come to their pack home on my own. It wasn't like it was far from the Institute, and it wasn't like I didn't have the app for ridesharing… it was just the principle of the thing.

I mean, I was all about feminism. I have rights. I have the right for the alpha I'm dating to pick me up himself and not have to figure out transportation on my own. It's really simple, basic stuff.

Was he hideous? Was that why Sabien and Kain hadn't ever shown me a picture of him? How would a hideous alpha end up in a pack with the twins? Sabien and Kain were beautiful men. They were stupidly pretty, golden perfection. How could they possibly end up with someone that looked like the human equivalent of a blobfish?

Whatever, I wasn't shallow. I cared about more than what an alpha looked like. There were other things that mattered. Maybe Sabien and Kain got with Brutus because he was rich.

What was I going to do if Brutus was awful?

What if he had the personality of a stale graham cracker? What if he was rude to waiters and watched podcasts of bald incels who wanted to show off their weird orange Bugattis and how much they hated women?

Would my budding love for Kain and Sabien be enough to survive Brutus?

I had to stop spiraling. Maybe I should take Nyle's advice and think positively, or whatever he'd said. Besides, I hadn't even met the alpha. There was no point in panicking. Yet.

I stood in front of my scent matches' pack house as if I didn't know how to operate a simple doorbell. Come on, it isn't even like I'd never been here before. I could do this.

I rang the doorbell and braced myself. I would *not* make a face if Brutus turned up and had a weird birthmark, or six fingers or something. For Sabien and Kain's sake, I was going to be open-minded about this.

No one opened the door. Instead, a harsh buzzer sounded and then the door clicked open. A low voice from an intercom, partially hidden behind the mail slot stated, "Come to the room at the top of the stairs."

…Brutus wasn't even going to welcome me in?

What was up with this guy?

The front door opened up to the now familiar view of

their sleek, modern living room—not quite the gross stereotypical bachelor pad. No, their room held an enormous television. Though their sofa was black leather, it looked buttery soft. Beneath the pedestal coffee table was a rug that was a pristine white—the kind I'd never seen growing up because it would last approximately four minutes in my house before getting ketchup or yogurt stains. It was the kind of room that looked like it was selected by someone who knew something about interior design.

Come to think of it, this wasn't the type of living space I'd expected from the twins at all. Sabien would be more than happy to lounge on extra large bean bags and call it a day. Kain let himself get too stressed out with his responsibilities to have the mental energy to pick out beautiful furniture.

Was Brutus responsible for all this?

I walked up the grand staircase to the first room and swallowed nervously, before bracing myself. I mean, it was just a guy. Alphas were a dime a dozen, and nothing to get worked up about. Why should I let myself get freaked out by some man who probably couldn't even manage to put his laundry in the basket? Even if he *was* so damn mysterious.

Something told me that Brutus wasn't the type to leave his socks lying everywhere. No. There was something more to him.

As I stood there contemplating theoretical laundry, the door wrenched open.

I craned my head up to take him in—this alpha towered over me, and my jaw dropped.

Fuck he was fucking sexy.

Dark. Tall. *Perfection.*

Brutus had a raw sexual energy like nothing I'd ever seen before. He was magnetizing, drawing me in. He was a bear of a man. The diesel version. Broad chested, and big everywhere. Thick biceps. Brutus wore his shirt unbuttoned, revealing chest hair sprinkled across firm pectoral muscles.

What does that feel like? Is it coarse? Or silky smooth?

All I wanted was to run my hands all the way down his chest.

There was something rugged and wild in him, like I was staring at a beast in a man's body. It was as if someone had taken the power of a tsunami or a hurricane, and crammed it into a human package named Brutus.

I could feel the weight of Brutus' attention on me. He looked up and down my body. Slowly, dragging his eyes across every inch of me, along my thighs, brushing across my chest, staring into my eyes. His expression was so heated and intimate he might as well have ripped my clothing off with his gaze.

He smirked as if he liked what he saw.

Boy, that little curve of his lip heated me up inside. Something in my lower belly clenched in anticipation.

Brutus had definitely noticed the way I was looking at his body. That I was *still* looking at his body.

He approached me with slow measured steps, his eyes on mine the entire time. As he came closer, his subtle scent wafted close. Sweet and floral. Light, but mouth watering, and drawing me in. He smelled like a banana.

Of course, his scent would be something shaped like a phallus— this alpha reeked of big dick energy.

"Baby, if you want to feel me, you don't need to ask." He grabbed one of my hands in his much larger grasp and pulled it against his chest. His very hard, very broad chest.

There wasn't an inch of give or softness to be found. The planes of his chest were nothing but a firm expanse of sculpted muscle.

I stroked along the fine hairs across his chest, and they were baby soft and springy against my fingertips. I rested my palm flat against his warm chest, not wanting to move away.

Brutus used one finger to tip up my chin, so I was staring straight into the heat of his dark eyes.

"Do you want to kiss me?" His voice was a purr.

My lips parted open, and my brain went blank, making an unhelpful BRrrRrrRRRRRRrrhhhhhhhh noise, like stupid static.

Uh. Yes.

Brutus' lips were plush for a man's and inviting me in.

Definitely yes.

But I couldn't figure out how to turn my thoughts back on in order to articulate myself. All I could manage was a small nod—but that was enough. Brutus laced his fingers in the hair at the back of my neck and pulled me in, leaning down until his luscious lips met mine.

God, his kiss lit me on fire.

His mouth was commanding, demanding entry. Demanding that I submit to him—something that I was all too happy to do.

Brutus wasted no time deepening the kiss. It was pure passion—as if I'd jammed my tongue into an electric socket and slathered myself in warm honey all at the same time. The way that his tongue danced against mine, brushing against me, claiming me with such exquisite friction.

He was going to make me lose my mind. Already my thoughts were spiraling out of control.

Brutus was addictive, I'd barely had a taste and already I was drunk on him. All I knew was that I needed him closer. He'd slid his arm around my waist and into my hair, and I needed him to hold me tighter. To hold me and never let me go.

Brutus grabbed me, rough. Pulling me against him. Squeezing into the soft flesh of my waist, his fingers bit into my skin like he couldn't get enough.

I was lost in his kiss. His lips were fierce against mine and I was blissfully turning into melted butter, as I leaned into that sizzling hot body. My thoughts were swirling, out of control. Whirling and wild. The room was spinning though I was stone-cold sober, as his kisses made me feel like I was untethered to my body and floating off somewhere into the ceiling, all the while I was falling hard into the pools of his dark eyes.

Each movement against my lips, each harsh scrape of his tongue, exploring the depths of my mouth, tasting me deep. Each touch made me want to lose control. All I wanted was him closer. So much closer.

Brutus held me tight against his body, and I could feel him, hard against my stomach.

Yes. I was his for the taking.

I could feel hunger in the way that he held me, in the way that his hands bit into me and clutched me against him so tightly. Every touch was a demand, and there was something about Brutus that made me want to give in to every one of his desires. It made me want to submit to him.

His fingers skimmed just underneath the hem of my blouse, tugging the fabric up, baring my stomach to his gaze. His fingers brushed against the slight curve of my belly, up along my ribcage, until soft touches skimmed against the lower curve of my bra.

His touches were making me lose my mind—I wanted more of him. I had to feel more of him.

Reaching back, I unfastened my bra, pulling it and my blouse up and over my head. Tossing it down to the floor. I stood before him half naked, forcing myself not to fidget under the force of his full and unwavering attention.

Brutus palmed my breast, cupping the tender flesh, running his fingers along my nipple. Teasing the peaks until they stiffened under his caresses.

"Are you ready to be my good girl?" Brutus slid his hands down my body to rest on the waist of my pants, by the button of my jeans.

His words were a drug—I think I was ready and willing to

do anything that he told me. Anything to get closer to the promise of more.

Every inch of this man's body screamed sex. The fluid way that he moved made it clear that fucking him would be phenomenal. I didn't want to wait to test it out.

I took a steadying breath before flicking the button open and sliding the jeans all the way down. Brutus followed every movement, watching each inch of skin I revealed to him.

"Get on the bed and spread those legs wide."

I could feel it the moment that feminism started to drain away from my body. Did I think that I should submit to a man and debase myself … No.

But did I want to be Brutus' good girl? Oh, *fuck yes.*

I bit my lip, as I felt slick dripping down my legs. He'd barely touched me, and I was so ready for him.

Brutus' bed was king sized, with black sheets, so smooth they looked like they were ironed. Taking a deep breath for courage, I turned and got on the bed, crawling to the center. I lay down, feeling the silky sheets against me. Slowly, I relaxed, letting my thighs fall open. Warmth pooled in my lower belly as Brutus stared at my pussy, not taking his eyes off me once as he moved toward me.

Then finally, he was putting the weight of his hard body on mine. Brutus reached between my legs. His index finger found my clit and started massaging me with the perfect circular rhythm to make me lose control. But just as I was on the cusp of coming, his fingers drifted lower, toward my other hole.

Without making the conscious decision to do so, I squeaked and pulled away from him.

"What's the matter, Love? You don't want all of your holes stuffed? Don't want your alphas to own every inch of your body?" His dark eyes were trained on my face, watching my face for every change in my expression.

"I've n-never…" I tried to take in a deep breath, but it just came out as a shudder.

"That's alright, Love. I'll ease you into everything. We don't have to play back there today."

Then Brutus' palm was on my clit, grinding down.

My back arched off the bed as I gripped the sheets, desperate to hold on to something. I whimpered, helpless against the onslaught of pleasure.

Brutus slid a finger against my entrance.

"That's it, you're fucking drenched for me."

As Brutus praised me, even more slick dripped down my thighs. I'd never been wetter in all my life.

Brutus moved off my body, just long enough to undo his belt and tug off his pants, freeing his cock.

My lips parted at the sight of it. While Brutus might not be as girthy as the twins, his cock was longer by far.

I'm in serious danger of getting dicked to death by all these massive cocks—which honestly is not the worst way to go.

Brutus slid his cock against my entrance painting my clit, as if his dick were a paintbrush. Back and forth, he teased me with just the tip. Giving me just a taste of the pleasure to come.

He rocked against me without giving me what I needed, until I couldn't take it anymore.

"Please," I whimpered, sliding my legs open further so that he knew exactly what I needed.

Brutus repositioned himself until I could feel him prodding me. With one thrust, he dove inside of me. Taking me deep. His hips were flush against mine, grinding against my clit.

He pulled out slowly, letting me feel every inch, drawing almost all the way out before fucking into me again. Over and over again, in a delicious rhythm.

The pressure, the warmth of his skin, the friction of his cock against my walls—it was all so *good.*

I wrapped my legs around his hips, pressing closer. Desperate to have more of him. My pussy clenched and more slick gushed down my thighs.

"Soak my cock, little omega. That's my good girl."

Brutus grabbed me, right by the neck, forcing me to look into his eyes. His pupils were blown wide with lust as he stared at me with a hunger I could feel all the way down to my bones.

"You take me so well. This pussy was made for me. Made to take all of me." He slammed his cock into me, brutally hard, fucking into me deeper.

I groaned.

The bliss took over until it felt like I was melting into pure pleasure. I didn't want to be a hard-working student on top of all her academics, I didn't want to be strong and at the top of my game. I didn't care about my rigid academic expectations. The only rigid thing that mattered anymore, was already moving inside of me.

I just wanted Brutus to fuck me until I couldn't think anymore. Just feel.

Brutus rested his big hand around my throat, squeezing gently. He leaned into my ear to whisper. "I want to control the air you breathe. I want you to know that every breath you take belongs to me."

That is incredibly toxic and I should not get off on that.

My clit was throbbing in response to his words. Because she was nothing but a stupid fucking cunt.

I gasped, forcing myself to pull in steady wisps of air, around the bulk of Brutus' bear-like hand. The light pressure around my neck made everything more intense.

I was nothing but feeling, and the sensations, and that hard slide of massive cock. The only thing I wanted to be was Brutus' good little omega.

Without warning, I came. Violently. Bursts of sharp pleasure erupted out of my core, rocketing down my spine like lightning. White hot pleasure coursed through each limb, shuddering through the length of my entire body.

In the aftershocks, I was nothing but a melted puddle where an omega used to be. I felt loose and unwound. If I wasn't careful I was going to melt straight into the bed.

Brutus had rocked into me in circular motions when I was coming, helping to draw out my orgasm. Now he picked up the pace until he was slamming into me. His rhythm was brutal. His balls slapped against my ass again and again. Diving into me so hard that his thrusts were shifting me up the bed. The whole time, he had his hand against my throat—not exerting any pressure, just holding me there, possessively.

Brutus grunted and thrust into me sharply. His knot thickened and swelled, locking his cock inside me.

Grinding against me, Brutus' cock pulsed. Throbbing deep within me. Warmth flooded my lower belly as he filled me up.

Wrapping his arms around me carefully, Brutus flipped us, laying me down carefully against his chest. He ran his warm hands in soothing patterns down my back.

Walking into this room, I was a bundle of anxiety. If I hadn't been so distracted by worrying about Brutus, I would be worried about my essay due in three days, or my online math test next week. Now, I felt oddly removed from all of those worries. Like, obviously they were still there. I was still going to finish my studies—I wasn't unhinged. But all of my focus shifted just enough that the weight of the worries wasn't pressing quite so heavily on me anymore.

I'd been a bundle of nerves—until Brutus fucked every single bit of tension and apprehension right out of my mind.

Maybe being an omega and getting a good dicking might even be better than working at a small desk job?

Woah now.

No need to get crazy.

Brutus' fucking was dangerous. He'd only dicked me once and I was halfway ready to toss my dreams in the trash and throw myself into his arms, without him even asking for it.

But honestly, if any dick was worth throwing away months of strenuous academic endeavor, piles of essays and readings—it was Brutus'.

CHAPTER 26
KAIN

A SURGE of pleasure hit me hard, until I was practically smacked upside the head with it. I turned to my twin. "Is that?"

"Yup." Sabien didn't look surprised at all to sense the scorching intensity of that raw physical attraction flooding the bond—which obviously could only mean one thing.

"When did their date start? Like fifteen minutes ago?"

Sabien nodded as he sprawled across the sofa with his feet up on the arm rest. "Are you really surprised? Do you remember how long it took for Brutus to get the two of us into his bed?"

That was a fair point. Brutus was one of those guys who knew exactly what he wanted and then went after it immediately. "You don't think that he's rushing Chloe—"

"No. Have you *seen* Brutus? He's hot as fuck."

He was.

It wasn't even really fair. My brother and I were also decently hot. Hell, Titus was so hot that he had the whole Institute drooling over him. But it was Brutus who had that raw animal magnetism that seemed capable of bending the whole world to his whims. Everything he ever wanted was delivered straight to him on a silver platter. Lucky for us, Brutus only ever wanted two things: a hot pair of twins and now Chloe.

"So..." Even though I knew without asking what the answer was, I felt like I still had to ask it. "Does this mean that you've forgiven him?"

The only reply my brother deigned to give me was chucking a sofa pillow straight at my head.

CHAPTER 27
BRUTUS

FUCK.

Why hadn't the twins warned me that our scent match was a redhead?

I had been ready to accept whatever omega the Valentine Division and their high tech scientific catalogs found for us. Blondes were obviously hot. I wouldn't complain if we ended up matched to a blonde girl. Dark haired girls were lovely. I found them to be alluring—their eyes always seemed brighter, framed against the deep hue of their locks.

But nothing got me bricked up like a redhead.

It might not be politically correct for me to say that I found redheads exotic, but fuck it. I want what I want.

Originally, I had planned our first date together differently. Obviously I'd wanted to assess her myself—this little omega who had captivated my twins. She might have proven herself academically… obviously there was enough attraction to entice the twins. But I had never even seen the girl.

Yes, biologically or mythically, or however you were meant to call it… I'd always assumed that we would end up with our scent match. How could any other omega compare?

But now that her identity had been revealed, doubts started trickling in.

The choice of our omega was the most important one that my pack would ever make. Even if our scent match was the omega we would be most compatible with… what if she was just a bitch? What if our personalities clashed?

I'd never met the girl, for all I knew she was convinced that the earth was flat and that our entire house should be repainted in neon pink and sparkly shit. What if she was the type of girl that crossed all of our boundaries and played the victim, while pitting my pack-mates against one another to win her affection?

This was our happiness at stake.

There was literally no other choice our pack would make that was as important as the omega we chose to bond. We didn't have to end up with our scent match. If it turned out that being with her would harm us, then the twins and I would have to have a serious talk.

It was a shame that I'd waited to meet her until after the twins had already gotten attached. I had to decide for myself if she was a good fit for the pack.

But Chloe Stryker was a fucking siren. Tall and lithe. With fine and delicate features and luscious curves.

Then there was her scent. Her decadent smell had burrowed itself into my mind, replacing my thoughts with sugary insanity.

She smelled so fucking amazing—like being plunged heart first into a crème brûlée. Chloe was so sweet and ripe. Honeyed and innocent.

My instincts took over, overpowering me with the need to *possess* her.

I couldn't think, I could barely even breathe until I had Chloe spread out and panting beneath me.

She was the fairest petal on a dainty flower and I had to

pluck her up. Take her for myself before anyone else could take her from me. From the three of us.

So maybe I fucked up. I'd wanted her too badly. The moment I saw Chloe, all that I knew was that I had to have her.

I had never felt this way before. Even with the twins, I'd spent time… albeit not much time… determining their habits and personality before I claimed them as my pack.

Now she was naked and knotted beneath me. Panting and catching her breath, making those perky tits jiggle. Her breasts were a nice handful, with perfect buds of rosy pink nipples.

Her soft thighs were wrapped around me, like warm silk.

Every inch of her body was perfection, and I could happily spend every moment of the rest of my days right here—lost in smooth skin and the give of her tender flesh.

Watching her half lidded eyes look up at me in pure exhaustion had me coming again. Another jet of my cum flooded into her. Locked deep inside of her with my knot, so that not even a drop of my essence could escape.

Well, fuck it.

I wasn't quite sure what kind of omega Chloe was. I might not know what she was like. There was only one thing that was clear.

Whoever she was, Chloe was mine.

CHAPTER 28
CHLOE

ALRIGHT. So Brutus had just gone and blown out my back, rutting into me like there was no tomorrow… and now, we were going to put our clothes on and go out on a date like nothing had happened?

Well, okay.

A date actually sounded pretty nice right now.

Brutus was proving himself to be the perfect gentleman, now that I'd met him properly and we'd exchanged bodily fluids. When we got into his car, he opened the door for me and everything.

He had a much nicer car than the one that the twins shared. The interior seats were leather, and Brutus showed me the buttons I could press if I wanted to turn on a seat warmer or cooler.

The ride was fairly short, just long enough to figure out which button controlled what, and to enjoy how the seat did some fancy shit that made my ass icy cold. Then Brutus stopped.

We were in the parking lot in a generic shopping plaza. Behind us was a grocery store with an elderly lady coming out of the sliding doors, pushing her cart that seemed to be loaded with cat food and bags of chips.

Honestly, if my guess was correct about Brutus being the one responsible for all the expensive furniture in the pack house, I was a bit surprised about the date location.

It's not like I'm some great connoisseur of relationships, but the grocery store just seemed like an odd choice for a first date.

Brutus opened the door for me, and all of a sudden he was standing before me. Right there and so close.

I bit my lip, taking all of him in.

Even fully clothed, with all of that glorious chest hair and the vast expanse of his muscular body fully covered, Brutus was magnificent. His very being exuded sex and raw masculinity—he was dangerous. I swear, being in close proximity was like a chemical reaction, turning me on and melting my thoughts into a giddy mess.

I was a shaken bottle of champagne, fizzy and exhilarated around him.

"Ready for more already, Love?" He leaned in closer, close enough that I was surrounded on all sides by his sweet bannana scent as he whispered into my ear, "keep looking at me like that and I'll have to fuck you again in the back seat."

My mouth dropped open.

Uhhh. That didn't sound like a bad thing? Getting fucked versus whatever he had planned for me in the grocery store.

But like he could read my thoughts, Brutus winked as he took my hand, leading me away from the tinted windows and the comfortable leather privacy of his car.

I tried not to pout as I followed Brutus to a little salon just past the grocery store.

Inside was surprisingly elegant. A delicate crystal chandelier hung from the ceiling. An ornate silver frame surrounded hundreds of rose blooms, artfully arranged together. A pink neon sign declared that this salon was 'Polish and Bliss.'

"Brutus, it's been too long!" A short man with bright purple hair sat up straight from where he was lounging. The man walked up to Brutus with a smile that was too wide and too enthusiastic. He walked all the way to Brutus, clasping his free hand in both of his. "What can I do for you?"

"Two mani pedis with the works, Fernando."

"Only the best for you, honey." The purple-haired man turned around hustling to the back of the store, presumably to fetch that 'best' for his 'honey.'

Something sharp and prickly that I didn't even know existed, reared its ugly head from somewhere deep within my omega hive mind.

It was ridiculous and territorial. I had to fight against the urge to start rubbing my scent glands all over Brutus and hissing at this intruder like a strung-out ally cat.

This other man hadn't even done anything that seriously hinted that he had plans to take my Brutus away.

Woah now.

Since when was he *my* Brutus? I'd just met the guy today.

From the moment the other man had touched my scent match, I'd gone very still. I was an ice sculpture, with cool anger thudding through my veins.

Though I hadn't said a word, Brutus had picked up on the tension. He gave my hand a gentle squeeze, pulling me in closer to the bulk of his body.

"Is my girl getting jealous?" Brutus teased in a low voice.

I couldn't answer him. I was so tense it was overwhelming. Especially since I knew that I was over-reacting, and that my hormones were just acting up. Yet, despite having read about these reactions in a dusty corner of my text books, here I was experiencing it for the first time. Knowing that it was just a part of being an omega didn't make me any less lost in it.

I didn't want to admit that I felt jealous. It wasn't fair. Brutus wasn't doing anything wrong. I couldn't just meet him for a first date and then start making feral noises at the salon staff, just because they were doing their jobs.

Yet still. Seeing that short little man touching *my* alpha made me want to tear my hair out, drop to the floor and cry myself to pieces… which would be awful for my hair, and fuck up the make up I'd put on for the date. It wasn't an option.

Brutus dropped a kiss on the top of my head. "I'm surprised you're jealous, now… with my cum dripping out of you. But I'd be happy to remind you that I only want you. There's no one else for me, Love. Just you and the twins." Brutus leaned closer to me, with his low seductive voice… with sex dripping from every word. "If you need me to *remind* you. Wherever you'd like, whenever you'd like. I'll remind you that you're mine."

Something about his deep voice pierced straight through my anxiety, settling over it like a warm blanket, until my fears were able to settle like an alligator sinking back into the still water.

My cheeks were heated with embarrassment, but I forced myself not to show it. Being a little bit rabid and defensive of my alpha was completely natural. Especially now, as things between us were so new.

As long as I didn't pull any truly deranged shit—like rubbing my scent to mark the nail clippers and polish used by Brutus—I still had a chance of walking out of this date without truly embarrassing myself.

Fernando walked back holding a basket of manicure supplies, with another one of those wide smiles that I irrationally hated. He beckoned over a coworker, who was younger, somehow even shorter but with less vibrant hair, pointing to one of the big chairs with a sink at the bottom.

The two men started fussing with the sink and the supplies, filling the basin with water. Then, they were pointing to the chairs, indicating that the two of us should sit.

I walked closer, side-eyeing Brutus to figure out what I was supposed to be doing.

He'd settled into the chair in front of the younger coworker, pulling off his socks and shoes, revealing feet that were big, hairy and somehow perfectly formed. Just like the rest of him.

I sat next in the chair next to him, in front of that little fucker Fernando, copying how Brutus began pressing buttons on the chair to turn on the massage function, and how he'd dipped his toes into the water.

"Have you never gone to a nail salon before?" When he saw me nod, Brutus smirked at me. "Perfect, I got one of your firsts, taking you here."

Oh God, that man lit my cheeks on fire. I risked a quick glance to Fernando to see if he was paying attention to our conversation. But he seemed to ignore me, fussing with the water in the tub. Fernando put in some blue powder that smelled like lavender and immediately made the water begin to bubble.

The warm water around my feet and the soothing scent of lavender in the air were enough to soothe my frayed nerves. Or maybe it was the fact that Brutus barely took his eyes off me, even when he was being massaged and scrubbed. The nail technician took out some tools and began to prod at Brutus' toe nails.

Brutus paid him enough mind to let him know that he wanted his nails "squoval shaped," whatever that meant. I swear I'm not dumb. At this point they weren't even using real words. Was everyone here in on it? Were they all just fucking with me?

When Fernando asked me what nail shape I wanted, I wasn't about to tell him that I had never thought about the shape of my nails before in my entire life, so I just said, "same as him," jerking my chin towards Brutus.

Then Fernando handed me an entire book of different colors that I could pick to paint my nails. There were way too many color options. I settled on a pale pink that looked pretty, without flipping too many pages. This whole process started to feel like a bit much—that is until Fernando started to rub my feet.

The foot massage was making me forget all about the fact that I was pissed at Fernando. He sort of was really good at finding all the tense spots, deep within the arch and at the corner of my heels, and then soothing all my discomfort away —he was doing such a good job at it that I wasn't even mad at him anymore.

After a bit, I got comfortable enough to have a conversation with Brutus, right in front of the nail tech who was probably–definitely not Brutus' secret lover. "Why did it take so long before I could see you? Why were you okay with the twins' plan to hide you away from me?"

"Were the twins acting like I'm the big bad wolf, here to abduct their little red omega to ride her?" Brutus was smiling at me in a way that was admittedly a little predatory. There was a small gleam of hunger in his expression whenever he looked at me, that made a thrill of anticipation slither down my spine.

With Brutus, everything he said felt like it was weighed down with the heavy promise of sex.

"They never mentioned you, like you were some dark secret."

Brutus pressed his back harder against his seat and closed his eyes for a moment. I couldn't quite blame him, this was rather nice.

There were rose petals floating around in the basin that I was starting to think of as my feet's personal little whirlpool. Fernando had pulled out hot rocks... and I don't know if I just had been living under a rock or something because I had no idea how good a massage like that felt. The heat of the rocks was cutting through all the tension I didn't even know I had. This felt amazing, even when they had started sugar scrubbing each foot, which was ticklish as hell. Then he took a file, and expertly started to shape my nails.

"The twins knew that I would seek you out on my own time." Brutus' eyes were closed, with a look of pure distilled relaxation on his face.

The way that Kain and Sabien left Brutus to do whatever he liked, they sort of treated him like he was the pack lead. But he wasn't. Officially, it was Kain who was the leader of the pack.

However, it was obvious who the dominant alpha was.

It was also pretty clear that neither of the twins would be able to get Brutus to do something that he didn't want to do. The only way that someone else was running their pack was if Brutus himself wasn't interested.

"Why didn't you want to be pack lead?" I thought I had a decent understanding of how the pack hierarchies worked; I'd aced the quiz on it and everything. The packs chose a leader who would make decisions and have the final authority on all pack business.

At home, it was obvious that Father was the pack lead. Someone just walking into our house without knowing a single thing about any of us would be able to figure it out immediately. Father seemed born for the role.

"I would be an awful choice as pack leader. Kain is in charge because he actually gets shit done. He makes the appointments, pays the bill, checks the mail. All that important stuff." Brutus was scrutinizing the way his nail tech was filing his nails. I don't know what exactly he was looking at—they sort of looked just like they did when he first walked in, only a bit shorter now.

"You don't care about taking charge?"

"No Love, I only care about fucking." There was no smirk on Brutus' face now, no hidden innuendo. He was telling the truth. "Kain's the obvious choice. If he didn't look exactly like his brother I would deny that the two of them ever shared a uterus. Sabien's the unfortunate appendage that Kain was born with. Now we're both stuck with him."

I noticed that Brutus' jaw tensed, though he acted like talking about Sabien wasn't bothering him at all.

"Do you really find Sabien that bad? Or is this all because of that sandwich incident?" I'd talked to Kain about the weird tension between the rest of his pack. All Kain knew about it was that he wasn't sure how it started; just that it had something to do with a sandwich—presumably, someone who wasn't supposed to eat it? If I didn't have so many siblings with a history of stealing my food, I'd say that this was all blown out of proportion. But honestly, sometimes you just had to stand up and protect your ham and cheese. Even from loved ones.

"Sabien's always been a bit of a twat when he's left unchecked. The sandwich was the last bit of drama that broke the camel's back." Brutus drummed his fingernails against the arm rest once before shaking his head, as if he had to bring up something unpleasant. "He called me, when the two of you were... *together.*"

Oh yeah.

Shit.

How exactly does one explain the need to finish an essay while an engorged penis was locked inside of one's vagina? In order to stay on top of all my coursework, I was just trying to have good time management. Should I say that it was my attempt at multitasking? No. That just sounded insane.

"I just wasn't expecting it. You know, the whole being stuck there thing. Waiting."

"Was that your first time with an alpha?" Brutus frowned.

"Yeah… that had been my first time…" My voice trailed off a bit.

I'd gotten comfortable around Fernando (he'd worked some kind of voodoo magic on my feet, at this point I wouldn't blame anyone for wanting to get a manicure from him), but that didn't mean that I was ready to outright talk about losing my virginity, right in front of him.

Luckily, Brutus was able to read between the lines.

"Sabien? Not even Kain? Well that's unfortunate. You picked the brother who has all the finesse of a jack hammer." He sighed deeply, shaking his head. "Did he even get you off?"

"Uhh." Did he?

I tried to think back. I definitely remember enjoying it… I know that Kain made me orgasm multiple times… but did Sabien?

Brutus seemed to take my non-answer as an answer. His expression darkened, and he sat straighter in his massage chair. "Don't worry. I'll sort him out."

Brutus pulled his hand away from his nail tech, Fernando junior or whatever, and examined his cuticles like a sovereign Lord examining his lands and titles. Satisfied, he stretched out his other hand, to be massaged and manicured. "You should be graduating soon."

"Yeah." It was less than a month and a half at this point. Just a few weeks away, really.

"After you're done with those Institute dorms, what do you think about moving in with us?"

My mouth dropped open a bit. Was Brutus asking me to move in? On the first date?

I don't know what it was about him… if the twins had asked me I probably would have felt love bombed, or like things were moving too fast.

With Brutus, all I felt was flattered.

Instinctually, my omega hive mind was doing giddy cartwheels and fist pumps. I had to rein it way in, before I leapt out of my massage chair and started running excitedly around the room and started bouncing off the walls like some rabid squirrel.

I felt like my insides were all filled with helium, and I was about to float straight into the puffy clouds with the men of my dreams.

Hold the fuck on. I needed to actually think about this.

"You want me to live with you?"

"Yes." His voice was dark and seductive, and I was embarrassed to say that at the moment, I was ready to agree with anything he asked me. "I want you to be my girl. Take my name." Brutus was staring right at my lips, like he wanted to kiss me, to take me, right here on this massage chair… in a nail salon that was next to a grocery store. "Join my Fanny pack."

"Wait. Excuse me. The what pack?" Was this some kind of joke? That was not even a real last name. Was it?

But Brutus frowned, completely serious. "The Fanny pack. Did Kain and Sabien never mention their last names? Kain Fanny? Sabien Fanny?"

Had I slept with the twins without even knowing their last names?

Apparently yes.

"You don't mean…" Please let this be some sort of misunderstanding. But all the cheerful bubbly endorphins within me were freezing into ice in my veins. Something dropped, deep in my stomach as my entire body started to tremble. "That's not the pack name." Please let this be some sort of misunderstanding.

"We're the Fanny pack." Brutus' gaze darted around my face and the way I was struggling to stop myself from having a full on panic attack.

This was not real. I did *not* just go from feeling the

happiest I could ever remember feeling, to being right on the verge of hyperventilating.

I could *not* be known as the omega of the Fanny pack.

Absolutely not.

"If it's the twin's name that's bothering you, we can come up with solutions. It's not exactly unheard of for packs to take the last name of the alpha who isn't the pack lead."

I took a deep breath to calm myself down.

I was falling in love with these men; they were my alphas. I'd been on the cusp of telling Brutus that yes, I wanted to move in with them. Yes, I wanted to be his, and everything that came with it.

It didn't make sense to throw that all away just because the pack name sounded a little silly. Especially when there was a reasonable course of action we could take about it.

But no. I should have known that it couldn't be that simple.

I didn't think that I could be more horrified, until Brutus told me *his* last name.

CHAPTER 29
CHLOE

GRADUATION WAS ON THE HORIZON.

The thought of graduating from the Institute had been my own little ray of hope, promising that I wasn't going to be drowning in quizzes and studying forever. In just a few weeks, I was going to get the instructions for my final exam. I didn't know when the countdown to the end of my classes had started weighing me down with its never-ending ticking and tocking like the countdown to a bomb.

I hadn't expected to like my scent matches.

Meeting all of them and realizing that I liked them, maybe even loved them, threw even more of a wrench in my plans. It was more emotionally devastating than if it turned out that we just weren't compatible at all. I had been emotionally prepared for a bit of heartbreak and to live my life alone in a studio apartment, living on my modest salary from my receptionist job—not to fall for my alphas.

Relationships made everything so much more complicated.

Brutus had spoken to me matter-of-factly about how things would be if I moved in with them, and about his plans for remodeling and personalizing my nest.

The whole concept of nesting was still weird to me. Yes, I'd been an omega for a while now. Yes, I knew that my moms and sisters had nests. But this was me, and I wasn't a fucking bird. I couldn't get the association of a bunch of little sticks surrounding a batch of eggs out of my head.

But that wasn't the point.

Moving in with my scent matches was a huge fucking deal.

It wasn't that I didn't want to be with them—I did.

The thought of a future without them made my limbs feel weak, as painful pressure built up in my chest—No.

I wasn't going to give up my alphas. But did that mean that I had to give up on my dream? After doubling my academic load at the Institute with my online classes, and nearly being done with them both, was I going to throw it all away? And to do what exactly? From what I'd seen with my sister, Rebel, it looked like all she did all day was her alphas... in various positions and pairings.

Wait. Honestly, that didn't sound awful...

But no. As much as I wanted to be with them, how could I give myself up in the process?

My mind was a dumpster fire, and nothing was helping. I wouldn't even mind an alpha interview during lunch right now, because it would take my mind off things. But even that had started to slow down. Titus hadn't texted me the contact of any new alphas in an entire week. Which was odd, because from the moment he'd come up with his hair-brained alpha interview scheme, he'd sent at least one, sometimes two or three alphas for me to interview a week.

Figures as soon as I actually wanted to do it, the interviews would dry up.

I got to class early.

I had all the space I needed to focus.

A few months back, I thought my academic year would be fucked after everyone realized I was related to the Stryker pack, but I'd used the incident to my advantage. Maybe I could have lied and said that there wasn't any connection to Titus, but it turned out that glaring at the other girls and hinting that I could ruin any chance they had with my brother worked just as well. The other omegas not only kept their distance, but treated me with a whispered reverence.

Which would have been perfect, except that I had already finished my assignments for the week. Now it was too much space.

I tapped my finger against my notebook, needing something to take my mind off everything. I looked behind me, to another omega seated a row behind me, who had also come in early.

"Good afternoon," I waved to her.

She turned bright pink and mumbled a tiny word, like a strangled and bastardized hello. Then the girl buried her head in her text book, blushing like it was her job.

Maybe I'd gone overboard with intimidating the other omegas. Was the threat of not being able to get with my brother really that scary? It's not like they could *all* get with him, anyway.

What-the fuck-ever. I was about to finish out my time at the Institute. It was a bit late for me to start thinking about friendships now. Besides, I had to keep my eyes on the prize. There was no doubt in my mind that if I failed my classes *now*, after I'd worked so hard at everything that I would have no other options but to simply die of embarrassment.

I just needed to find something else to take my mind off things.

Mindlessly, I grabbed my phone, tapping out a text to Titus.

Me: Are you even alive?

> Titus: Hey! I'm at the Institute. Meet me at
> our usual for lunch?

Oh?

So he was at the Institute right now? Titus wouldn't come by this way unless he had paperwork, or he was here to meet alphas.

I opened up my textbook to a chapter on condom textures, hiding my smile behind it. So which alpha was my brother meeting? Were things getting serious? There was nothing better than other people's love lives and drama, to take my mind off my own real-life problems.

An hour and a half later, I loaded down my lunch tray with a supreme steak burrito and a side of nachos with salsa. It looked amazing, and I was starving, having been in too much of a rush to make it to the cafeteria in time for breakfast.

To be completely honest, I was a little distracted as I walked out to my favorite lunch table. I had to keep looking at my lovely little burrito, promising it that I'd give it a good home—in my belly.

When I got to the table, I looked up to see Titus, happier than I'd ever seen him—and he wasn't alone. He was surrounded by three other alphas, standing close together… staring at each other with hearts in their eyes.

Wait… wait.

Wait one damn minute.

Did this mean that he'd actually chosen his pack?

My brother had his arms around a handsome alpha with dark wavy hair, and thick lashes framing emerald-green eyes —it was Nyle, the one alpha that I'd recommended to Titus. The only man out of the dozens I'd interviewed that actually passed my red flag checklist and earned a glowing recommendation.

Titus had actually called me and asked me if I was being serious, after I'd texted him that he needed to snatch Nyle up, bond him and put a ring on it.

Huh. Titus actually took my recommendations seriously. Honestly, I suspected that Titus was using the alpha interviews as an excuse for me to go out and maybe get laid… but that didn't completely make sense, because the interviews didn't stop when I'd found my scent matches.

It was one thing to suspect that my brother cared about my opinion on which of the alphas at the Institute were decent and which ones were the human equivalent of diarrhea on a toilet seat, and it was another to realize that he'd actually taken my advice.

Nyle wasn't the only alpha I recognized.

Was that Simon?

I mean, alright. The heart wanted what the heart wanted. Who was I to be the judge of all that? Besides, from what I could tell, Simon was determined and earnest. He wasn't the sharpest crayon in the box, but he was emotionally regulated and definitely not a psycho.

Simon stood with his chest puffed out and chin held high.

Okay.

Good for you, Simon.

"Ah, there she is!" Simon exclaimed as soon as he spotted me. He held out his hand for me to shake, and I had to hurriedly lower my tray to the table. Simon took my hand in both of his, shaking it with enthusiasm, "I've got to thank you for your support in the pack interview process."

My mind drew a complete blank. What had the two of us even spoken about? All the interviews blurred together a bit.

Oh, shit.

Simon wasn't the alpha who'd gone army crawling through the Institute cafeteria to get me a sandwich, was he?

Whatever. If it got him noticed and a part of Titus' pack, no harm done.

"You're welcome." I smiled in reply, my gaze darting over to my brother in question.

Titus glanced pointedly to the alpha next to him.

Got it. Whoever was at my brother's side had the hots for Simon.

"Chloe, I'd like you to meet Arrow." Titus reached down and took Arrow's hand, "he's a good friend of mine."

A good friend, huh?

Fuck yeah.

Now, I remembered how I'd practically text screamed at Titus to man up and talk to this "friend" that he'd been clearly interested in.

I could immediately see why Titus liked him. Arrow was handsome, like all of the other alphas Titus had me interview... but there was something alluring about Arrow.

Maybe it was the buzz cut that drew attention to his doe-like brown eyes. They were soulful and deep, framed by exquisite long lashes. He had high cheekbones and thick and delicate lips, that were a dusky rose against his dark complexion.

Well... fuck. If I didn't have my scent matches, I would be tempted to go for Arrow as well.

Was there a way for me to give my brother a high-five and tell him *"nice"* without seeming disrespectful? There should be. Titus did good.

Even meeting him for just a brief while, I had a good feeling about Arrow. He seemed sweet, and he couldn't take his eyes off my brother for a second. I don't even understand why Titus would even have me do all of these interviews in the first place, the way that he was looking at Arrow with a dumb grin on his face.

Boys were just fucking dumbasses sometimes.

———

"Hey, I'll walk you back to class." Titus said, as I got up to throw the crumpled tin-foil (all that was left after a truly decadent burrito. Ten out of ten) in the trash and scurry back to my evening lectures.

Titus turned to Arrow, cradling that strong jaw in his hands. "I'll see you in a minute," he murmured before leaning down to give him a quick kiss, full on the lips.

Arrow nodded as he broke away from the kiss looking a little bit breathless. His eyes were wide, as he stared at Titus as if my brother was the best damn sight in the world.

Awwww!

I was so happy that my brother was happy.

Even if Titus was my brother, and I could remember all of his awful teenage years… all those gross sweaty hugs, the fermenting clothes that were always *near* but not *in* the laundry basket and the general rebellion against deodorant— I had to admit, my brother was an okay dude.

Once the two of us were around the corner and out of sight, I threw my arms around my brother. "I love your pack and I'm so fucking proud of you."

Titus wrapped his arms around me, squeezing tight.

"Thank you, Chloe." Titus let me go, clearing his throat as if that could distract me from the way that his eyes were welling up with emotion, and that he was right on the brink of crying happy tears. "I don't know what I was even thinking with Arrow… if you hadn't started bitching at me to talk to him…"

Bitching?

No. I was saving him from a lifetime of regret.

"Hey, I get it." I nodded at him.

There must have been some onions around here, because now my eyes were starting to get a little bit teary.

"Love makes everyone stupid." I shrugged. "Maybe because love itself is stupid. But as long as you are happy, and you get there eventually, who gives a shit?"

CHAPTER 30
CHLOE

"COME ON. Pick up. Please, please please." I had the phone jammed up against my ear as tight as it could go. Honestly, all of this might just be part of the test. Maybe this really was an accurate measure of my abilities as an omega. Maybe I should just hope for the best.

No. Fuck that shit. I had studied my ass off for the entire term. It wasn't fair that everything that I'd worked hard on for months was about to go straight into the trashcan over something as ridiculous and stressful as this tiny machine that could fit in the palm of my hands. Someone on the Omega Curriculum Development board must have been on some kind of acid-trip when they came up with this idea for our final exam.

After a mini-eternity, as the phone rang eight times, she picked up my call.

"Momma Rain! Do you know anything about keeping Tamagotchis alive?"

I could hear Momma Rain make an undignified sound, like she was covering up a snort. "Honestly, not at all. I baked a cake celebrating when Zane's tamagotchi battery finally died. Why would you want to keep one alive?"

"It's for my final. They gave me four of them. Four! They said it's supposed to mimic taking care of a pack."

"Oh wow. My final was totally different. I heard they changed things after the tragedy in two thousand thirteen."

"What tragedy? Wait, isn't that when the omega dorms got renovated?"

"Yeah, from the electrical fire caused by too many vibrators charging at the same time. They changed the final after that." Momma Rain's voice got muffled as she placed the phone down. I could barely make out what she was saying to one of my siblings. It was something about the ketchup being behind the pickle jar or something like that. "Sorry, so what was this about tamagotchis? They're supposed to mimic taking care of a pack? What do little robots have to do with a pack?"

That was exactly what I was wondering. No matter how hard I tried with them, nothing ever seemed to be good enough. I was about to pull out my hair. The final was fifty percent of my entire grade. After all of the reading I had to do on testicles and multiple orgasms and every single topic they made me read about, how was it fair that my grade came down to this?

I was supposed to watch these little robotic terrors all night. If a single one of them died, I would fail my final. That would have been bad enough under normal circumstances, but the tamagotchis that they had acquired for the omega final? They were something else. They must have gone into the code and altered them somehow, because there was no way that anyone would ever buy one of these things recreationally if they were as demanding as these four had been.

"All of them are hungry, and there are electronic poops everywhere." I was barely able to keep the hysteria out of my voice.

"Oh sweetie, I'm so sorry. That sounds awful. Did you try calling Rebel?"

"I think she's having a heat or something. She's not picking up. Everyone's number in her pack is going straight to voicemail." I was pacing now, with the phone jammed against my ear. I frantically pressed the buttons on the screen to give the little guy a bath *again*. But as soon as I finished it, two other screens lit up demanding more food.

How was this supposed to teach me anything? I was lucky that I had met actual alphas before this. If I hadn't… if I thought an actual pack of alphas was anything like this, all this test was teaching me was that I should seriously consider remaining single for the rest of my life.

"Do you have anyone who could help you out? In real life there is nothing wrong with getting support with your pack." Momma Rain's voice was empathetic, even as I heard the faint sound of something crashing in the kitchen and the screams of two of my siblings—was that Gunnar and Rowan?

"Yeah, actually…" That gave me an idea… a completely academically unethical idea, but I was desperate enough to take desperate measures. "I know who could help me out. Thanks Momma."

Once I got myself to the Fanny Pack house, the guys were all in shock when they saw me. It was obvious that I had been crying. My eyes felt itchy and splotchy. I knew from experience that they must be red-rimmed along with tear streaks that would not go away, no matter how many times I tried to brush them off my face. I thought that they might have been relieved to find out that I had working, functional tear ducts, and was capable of being vulnerable with them, but the mood in the house went somber fast.

Brutus held my face gently, rage burning in his dark gaze.

"Who did this to you?" Brutus' words promised vengeance and retribution. Someone or something had harmed his scent match and nothing would stop him until that harm had been paid out in blood.

Silently, I held up the four shitty little gadgets that had been plaguing me for hours.

All three of the guys leaned in closer, frowning.

"Are those tamagotchis? I didn't even know that they still made those. Why do you have them?" Kain's eyes narrowed as if I was holding a fistful of grenades.

"Wait, are these things the reason you're upset?" Sabien poked one of them warily, as if he was afraid that the little demon egg would give him an electric shock. "Why not just throw them all in the trash?" he muttered.

My lips trembled as I tried to hold back fresh tears. In a small voice, I managed to say, "They're for my final. I can't throw them away."

My scent matches blinked, staring at one another in confusion. Brutus' gaze flicked from my face to the egg-shaped gadgets in my hand, like he was having trouble making the connection why colorful bits of tech and plastic had the power to make me cry.

"These are for your final?" Kain asked, gently getting me to explain what the hell was going on.

"I need to take care of them. It's supposed to be like taking care of a pack, but this is too much." I was blinking back tears, and one electronic poop away from having a complete mental breakdown. "Please. I just need to pass my final."

"So, these things… are supposed to be us?" Brutus narrowed his eyes at the tamagotchis, clearly pissed at the little machines that had *dared* to distress his scent match. But was that a good thing? *Did this mean that he wasn't going to leave me with all these electronic alpha egg-monsters?*

"It's alright, darling. We'll help you." Kain gently pulled the little machines from my tight grasp, handing one to each member of the pack.

I *thought* that handling a pack of men was easier than all of these tamagotchis, but the Fanny pack seemed hell bent on proving me wrong. Hypothetically, taking care of one egg-demon should have been easier than four—if I didn't have to micromanage the care that they were receiving from my scent matches.

Kain was button mashing and looked on the verge of having a full-on panic attack. Brutus was suspiciously calm. Clicking buttons on one of the tamagotchis without a care in the world. I narrowed my eyes, watching exactly what he was doing with it.

"Brutus! Stop disciplining it! You can't just discipline it five times in a row."

"Well, it needs to learn its damn lesson somehow." Brutus was snarling, and directing all of his big-dick dominant alpha energy on the tiny screen.

"It's a fucking robot-egg, not a submissive!" I buried my face in my hands as if that would make this nightmare just go away.

After Brutus reluctantly started to actually provide care instead of whatever kinky-shit he'd been attempting, I rushed to clean my tamagotchi for what felt like the hundredth time in the past hour.

"Stop giving it treats! He needs water!" I said to Sabien, before moving to check on Kain.

I looked up sharply at Sabien when he muttered darkly, "I'll give you water."

Sabien was literally holding the tamagotchi by the frail little chain, and was slowly lowering it into his cup of water. He stopped a millimeter away from dunking it under, when he noticed my scorching glare. I was mentally screaming at him, *don't you dare.*

Had he really been on the cusp of drowning one fourth of my final in his drink? What the hell? I swear to all the gods, old and new, if Sabien drowned my final, I wouldn't break up with him. I would talk the rest of the pack into helping *me* drown *him*.

Sabien sighed heavily, as he pulled the little robot out of the cup, acting as if asking him not to murder my final assignment was *such* a big ask. "Wait, what happens if you bring back a dead tamagotchi?"

"Oh. I'd fail. I would have to take all of my classes at the Institute over again next year." I didn't even look at him, as I eyed the happiness meter on my tamagotchi in concentration.

"Wait, seriously?" Kain's voice was so tight with tension, he sounded like he'd been strangled.

"Well, yeah. Why do you think I've been stressing out so hard?" I frowned.

Kain, Brutus and Sabien froze, before staring at one another in shock. They gave each other grim looks, as if they had all wordlessly agreed on something.

I guess that electronic pet sitting was a lot less funny, when failure could mean a whole year of being distanced from your scent match. Besides, if I had to spend another year redoing all of my coursework... just to face these little robotic demon pet spawn again, I'd lose my mind. If one of them died, I was going to lock myself straight into an insane asylum and get myself heavily medicated, because I was *not* going to deal with all that again.

The tamagotchi care did *not* go more smoothly now that my scent matches were actually taking the task seriously.

Tension and concentration was thick in the air. All three of my scent matches were each hunched over a gadget in silence in a way that was definitely going to end with them all having back and neck pain. I thought that we were past the worst of the drama, when the silence was broken by pure unadulterated panic.

"Shit. Shit. Shit. Google it! I don't think the screen is supposed to look like that. What the fuck is this? Is the battery low? Are you fucking kidding me? After I played with you and fed you dozens of times, YOU DON'T GET TO DIE!" Kain clenched his jaw as a vein in his forehead bulged in panic.

"It's okay! It's okay." I reassured Kain, brushing soothing patterns along his arm. If that didn't work, I was not above scent marking him to calm his ass down. "Look there. It's just sweat on the screen. The little alien thing is fine."

I didn't realize that the four of us, and our needy electronic charges made it through the night, until my concentration was broken by a familiar ringtone. I put my tamagotchi down, wiping the tiredness out of my eyes before bringing my phone to my ear. "Hello?"

"Hey, Chloe." Rebel's voice was hoarse and just a bit dreamy. She didn't even sound like she was fully out of her heat yet. "You called me? Like six times?"

"Yeah, I was panicked." I ignored a sound in the background that I was *not* supposed to hear, as one of Rebel's alphas whispered something that I immediately burned from my memory. "Rebel, how did you keep all of your tamagotchis alive?"

Rebel laughed. Straight up laughed in the face of the trauma that those egg shaped terrors caused. "You mean the final? I didn't even try. I reset half of them the next morning."

"You… reset them?"

"Yeah, my teacher Professor Davis was close to retiring. She barely graded anything. There was no way that she was going to manually click through hundreds of tamagotchis. She just looked at mine for like a second and saw that they were alive, before chucking them back into the box."

I swallowed. Forcing myself to take deep breaths. There was no way something that simple would have worked for me. I hadn't gone through all of that… for *nothing?*

"Chloe… you okay?"

"I'll call you back," I managed to mutter. I carefully placed my phone down without shattering it. I didn't make eye contact with the alphas who were all lying exhausted, and the stupid pile of happy tamagotchis in the center of their kitchen table.

I walked to grab a pillow from the sofa, grabbing it carefully. I dug my face into the soft fabric and screamed into it as loud as I could.

CHAPTER 31
CHLOE

CLEARING out my desk was making my eyes watery. It must be the dust in here or something. My workspace looked naked now that I had returned all of the textbooks. All that remained was a neat stack of graded essays and tests.

On top of the stack was a letter on fancy cardstock paper, informing me that I was the Valedictorian omega of my class.

I'd asked one of my professors point blank what I could do as a Valedictorian omega. She'd enthusiastically told me how it would open up doors for me to get introductions to high-status packs. Alphas working in the government, or even those with celebrity status tended to scope out the omega who'd earned the title of Valedictorian.

Yeah, the last thing that I wanted right now was to have to meet even more alphas. Helping Titus find his pack-mates had me meeting enough alphas to last a lifetime. Thanks but no thanks.

There were post-its everywhere—until now my life had been held together firmly by all of those bright bits of sticky paper. Each of them had dates and reminders of deadlines that had seemed so important to me.

Minimum 1k words—Due Tuesday!!!

Review chapter on suppressant overdose and accidental poisoning

It felt wrong to just throw them away… what was I going to do with them? I peeled off each post-it and made them into a neat little stack. They went right on top of the fancy Valedictorian letter. Now all that was left was to throw the stack into my suitcase with the rest of my things, and I would be officially done with my time at the Institute.

But where would I go?

Brutus had sent texts about how he was taking me nest shopping, whatever that meant.

Daddy-Lo texted me that he could get here in half an hour, just let me know when I wanted him to pick me up.

Yeah. I couldn't ignore this any longer.

I scrolled through my contacts to the only person who would be able to understand.

Me: Hey, I need to talk to you.

Me: Can you meet me at my dorm?

Kain: Alright, darling. I'll be there in twenty.

I held Kain's hand leading him through the hallways of the omega dormitory. It wasn't too packed right now. There were parties going on with families down in the cafeteria. But there were still some curious omegas lingering around, and they were definitely paying attention to the hot blonde alpha walking through their territory.

I caught one omega wave shyly at Kain. I might have been annoyed enough to snap at her to get her own alpha, or glare at her or something. But if Kain noticed her, he didn't show any sign of it.

That worked for me. I ignored the girl too.

As soon as the two of us were alone in my emptied out dorm, Kain pulled me into his arms, swinging me around in a circle.

"Congratulations on graduating. You busted your ass for this." Kain grinned at me with his boyish, charming smile. He was like sunlight, and golden warmth—he felt like home. As he wrapped his strong arms around me, hugging me tight, Kain leaned in close to my ear and whispered, "so proud of you."

I managed a weak smile in return.

Yay. Graduation…

"Brutus told me he invited you to live with us. Did you make your decision? Are you moving in with us?"

I felt like I couldn't breathe. Like all the air was sucked straight out of me as I slowly shook my head, no.

God, all I wanted to do was to tell him yes. I was going to move in with them. I was ready to join their pack and bond them… but it wasn't the truth.

Why did it feel like the earth was being ripped out from under me and I was falling?

Why did this feel like a goodbye?

The enthusiasm seeped out of Kain, like the slow leak of a helium balloon. What was worse was that it was all my own fault. I was the one who had stolen that enthusiasm away from him, and Kain had done nothing to deserve it. A part of me wanted to wipe the hint of sadness away from his brilliant blue eyes—the pain that I had put there.

But I had to do this.

"I just need some space. To think."

"But you're coming back to us, right? After you do what you need to do? After you have some time to figure this out?"

I didn't say anything. I couldn't say anything. This hurt too much.

Kain closed his eyes, and his voice went soft. "Are you breaking up with us?"

What?

Breaking up was the last thing that I wanted to do. Is that what I was doing? What the fuck was I doing?

No.

I couldn't lose them. That wasn't what this was about.

I shook my head violently. "I j-just..." I started sniffling, and my eyes burned with tears that were making everything blurry, forcing myself to get the words out before I lost everything. "I don't want to break up."

Suddenly, warm arms were all around me. Kain held me close, brushing comforting patterns up and down my back.

I pulled just far enough away to get a look at him. Though his expression was strained, like he was forcing himself to appear composed, he wasn't able to hide the pain in his eyes.

I hated this. I hated that I was the one who had hurt him, when Kain had been nothing but good to me.

One minute I was leaning in, drawn in to Kain's brilliant blue eyes—they were an ocean, and I was so damn thirsty... all I wanted was to drown in them... until my lips were inches away from his...

The next moment his lips were locked with mine. Pressing against my mouth, feverishly hot.

I moaned at his touch, ready to lose myself, forget all the shit that had come between us to just fucking feel him. Just that rough slide, the delicious friction as his tongue moved against mine.

The scent of chocolate was heavy in the air, decadent and demanding. Smooth and rich, there was nothing but his creamy scent all around me and it was the only thing I wanted.

It wasn't enough. I needed more of him.

I moved my hand under his shirt, needing to feel him. Sliding my palm against his warm skin, and the firm muscles tensing under my fingertips. I jerked his shirt up and out of the way.

Kain broke off our kiss, for long enough to rip his shirt off, in one smooth motion.

I didn't even have enough time to stare at the perfection that was his athletic torso before he was on me, pressing hot open-mouthed kisses against my neck, until I was sinking into the heat of him.

Kain slid his fingers under my shirt, brushing against the skin of my belly in feather-light touches that were driving me insane. The slow trails he was weaving across my body all felt like they were lighting me on fire.

Then Kain was kissing my neck roughly, sucking down hard and pressing his teeth right against my sensitive skin.

I whimpered—it was right where we could bond. All he had to do was press down just a little harder. If he would just bite me. Bite me. He was right there, so close and he could make me his.

But then Kain broke away from my neck, with a groan. His eyes were hooded with lust, his pupils dark with want.

"Tell me to stop." His voice was wild, frantic... as if he was as desperate as I was to burn down these walls that I'd thrown between us.

"Please..." my voice was high and breathless and filled with that same desperation. "Don't stop."

Kain gasped sharply before he was jerking off my shirt, unbuttoning my jeans and dragging them from my body.

My hands were behind my back, awkwardly reaching for my bra clasp. I'd barely unhooked it when Kain was tossing me down on my bed.

I moaned as he pushed his face right in between my thighs, laving at my pussy. He was *devouring* me. Kain lapped a path straight to my clit, as if my pussy was the sweetest cream and he was fucking *starving*.

Kain teased me, running one finger in a circular motion around my entrance, just how he knew I liked it, before sliding inside. Pressing against the walls of my pussy, finger fucking me roughly as he mouthed down harder against my clit and *sucked.*

Fuck.

My back arched off the bed. I shrieked as I came, bursting apart at the seams, with light sparks flashing across my vision. My pussy pulsed, vibrating in pleasure that shot across my limbs. Until I was left shaking with the ferocity of it, with my legs trembling uncontrollably.

Kain pressed one sweet kiss, gently right on top of my clit, before he stood upright. His heated gaze scorched my body as he unbuckled his pants, tugging them down roughly to free himself.

Kain wasted no time climbing over me on the bed, settling between my hips. With one rough thrust, he was inside me, all the way to the hilt.

Kain groaned, pulling his fat cock out of me, so I could feel every inch against my pussy, before diving back in. Hard. Creating a rough friction as he began to move.

This wasn't like the thoughtful, rhythmic lover I'd come to know and love.

No.

Kain was fucking me. Pounding into me wildly and out of control. Slamming into me so hard that each thrust knocked the flimsy bedframe against the wall. Even as his balls slapped against my ass. Over and over.

Until I was nothing but a whimpering mess beneath him, powerless. All I could do was spread my legs open wider to welcome each hard thrust.

He was fucking into me hard enough to break through to me, shattering all the excuses I'd hidden behind.

He fucked the truth into me—that I was his. That I was made for him.

Fucking me hard enough until I had no choice but to see it, too.

Then he groaned, pushing his cock deeper into me as his

knot thickened and swelled inside of me. His warm cum jetted deep inside of me, filling every empty space within me with everything he had.

As the two of us lay entwined together, a panting tangle of sweaty limbs, all of the words that had been jumbled up in my head suddenly sorted themselves out.

I looked into Kain's eyes and he was looking back at me with pure devotion… like I was a goddess, even after everything I'd put him through.

I took a deep steadying breath. "I don't want to lose you. But if I don't do this, I feel like I'm going to lose myself."

"I am yours." Kain kissed my knuckles sweetly, butterfly soft. "Take all the time that you need, as long as you come back to me."

I closed my eyes, as I nodded.

I wouldn't be able to do this if I could see the heartbreak written all across his face.

But I had to. I was doing this to become the best version of myself. I had to reach out and see if I could grasp my dreams.

Then why did it feel like I was ripping out my own heart?

CHAPTER 32
CHLOE

MILLER SMILE'S Dentistry was perfect beyond my wildest dreams. On the day of my interview, it was quiet. Patients sat silently in gray waiting chairs. The walls were an aesthetically pleasing beige, with clinical pictures of tooth decay and gum disease. They had an immediate opening. Dr. Miller told me that he thought I was perfect for the position.

It was going to be my first quiet desk job, and I was beyond ready to start. That morning, I brushed my teeth twice, which wasn't a job requirement, but just felt like the right thing to do. I took the first bus of the day, which left while the sunrise still left a colorful mix of pinks and oranges painted across the sky.

I was going to demonstrate my competence. Quietly. Leaving all of the drama behind me. I was going to show everyone that I was capable, and I didn't need this designation, hormones, and fancy omega scent in order to be a functional and contributing member of society.

In short, I was ready to kick ass at my desk job.

The dentist headed in, and I greeted him with a smile.

This was everything that I had ever wanted. I was finding my own way in the world.

"Good morning," I said in an enthusiastic voice, as Dr. Miller stepped up to the reception desk.

"Coffee, black with two sugars." He didn't even look at me.

"What?" The word just slipped out at his brusk tone. I knew what a coffee was, *obviously*.

Dr. Miller sighed loudly, and then actually turned to look at me for the first time. Only, he was glaring at me like I was an idiot. "There's a coffee mug down in the breakroom. Grab me a cup of coffee. Put two sugar packets in it. No milk or creamer. Bring it down to my office. Do you think you can manage that?" He said each word slowly, enunciating every-thing with contempt dripping from each syllable.

"Yeah, I got it." Turning away before my new boss could see how red I was turning.

Was this normal? Was I so wrapped up in the proper behavior of omegas that I wasn't able to fit into the real world anymore? I don't know, I was getting pretty good at clocking people as assholes. But none of the alphas I'd spoken to had been so *rude*.

Were people only being nice to me because they wanted to get into my hot brother's pants? Or my pants? Without the sex appeal, was I just not worthy of respect?

What was going on?

Alright. It was just my first day. Got off to a bad first impression with the boss man, but that wasn't the end of everything. I wasn't about to give up over one miscommuni-cation over a little cup of coffee.

Walking down the hallways, coffee cup in hand, I heard my coworkers mutter to one another. They were whispering, but not quietly enough that I couldn't make out their words.

"Poor little omega doesn't know what she's in for."

Part of me wanted to stop walking. To just give them a frosty glare. If one sharp look was enough to make the hot-blooded alphas back at the Institute quiver in their boots, it was probably enough to get beta women to stop whispering about me in ear shot.

I forced myself to keep walking as if I'd never heard them. They didn't think that I could handle this job because of my designation? Well, fuck them. I was Chloe Stryker. I'd put up with *months* of strenuous academic commitments to be here.

I wasn't about to let some jaded coworkers take that away from me.

I brought the cup all the way back to the dentist's office. Dr. Miller didn't say a word to acknowledge my presence, just grabbed the coffee and took a sip. Blatantly ignoring me. I hurried away. It wasn't like I was *avoiding* my new boss or anything. I, Chloe, the highest academic achiever in my cohort, did not *cower* in the face of rude dentists. It was just because of new job jitters. Or something.

It wouldn't kill him to say thank you.

At least I thought it wouldn't kill him. The weight of all that ego lodged in that big old skull might be killer. Especially since it seemed built like a jenga tower. Maybe one word of gratitude would be all that it took to make the whole thing come crumbling down and destroy him.

Maybe this was a common new-hire experience? Was it normal for employees to expect a little bit of hazing? That sounded like an excellent question for google once I got home.

Alright, now that the unpleasant coffee experience was over and done with, I was ready to work.

I returned to my post at the reception desk, armed with a smile and a killer shade of red lipstick.

My back straightened as the front door opened. Emma, the other secretary at the counter, was with another patient, so it was all up to me. The man walking in was a bit bedraggled, carrying himself with nervous energy. Could he be anxious to go to the dentist? I know that I had a hard time with the thoughts of needles in my mouth.

"I'm here for my eight thirty appointment." The man slid over his identification that read Ronald Brown.

I didn't need to look at my watch to know that it was long past eight-thirty.

"Let me confirm the availability with Dr. Miller." Over the weekend, I made flashcards with all of the protocols listed in the manual. I had it down to a science.

"I'm only fifteen minutes late. There was traffic on the highway."

Fifteen minutes my ass. Someone doesn't know how to do basic fucking math. I kept the smile on my face, though inside it was strained. "I completely understand, Mr. Brown. The policy just states that I need to check Dr. Miller's availability for late patients."

"My tooth is fucking throbbing right now. I took off work for this." Ronald clenched his bony hands into a fist. He reminded me of my baby brother when he was on the verge of a meltdown. Except that Rowan was a two-year-old. "I'm here for my appointment and you are just wasting time. Why can't you go and do your damn job?"

"I understand sir, just give me a minute to—"

He didn't even let me finish my sentence.

"What, are you stupid or something? If I didn't have to wait for you, I'd already be seeing the dentist by now."

My mouth was hanging open. The second I realized, I shut it with a snap.

"Sir, I need to confirm that Dr. Miller still has the availability to see you."

"What, are you a parrot? Got to repeat everything? If you weren't such a stupid fucking *cunt*, I'd be getting my teeth fixed right now." Not only was Ronald raising his voice at me, he leaned in so close that tiny flecks of angry spit landed right on my face.

"Does there seem to be a problem? Sorry love, it's Chloe's first day." Emma smiled at me with a smile that didn't quite reach her eyes. "Why don't you take a seat in the waiting area and I'll go let Dr. Miller know that you're here."

That was basically the exact same thing that I said. So why was this loser nodding and doing what Emma told him to?

When Ronald went in the back to his appointment, he flashed Emma a smile, before rolling his eyes at me. Ronald muttered, in a completely audible voice, that I was a stupid bitch.

Okay.

It wasn't my fault that he came in late.

My self reassurances that things could only get better were getting really strained.

Why did I think that working in a dentist's office would be a quiet position? Sounds carried perfectly all the way from the treatment room to the front desk. I could hear *everything*.

I tried not to flinch as one parent screamed at her kid and tried my best to tune out the sound of sobbing.

"Just stop crying. Stop it. It's making you drool more."

"It's going to hurt." The kid couldn't be older than four. She had sweet little pigtails and sparkly sneakers.

"You better knock that off, you hear me? It doesn't even hurt, he just needs to check you to fix your teeth."

All day, the noise would not stop.

I attempted to tune out the sounds of drilling, and the muffled sounds of kids screaming at the top of their lungs for long enough to focus on the next patient who had gotten to my counter.

I had imagined that Mr. Brown would be the worst patient of the day. Which was fine. I'd just knocked the worst out right away. It didn't take me long to realize that this was clearly not the case.

"What the hell do you mean that it costs one thousand, three hundred and sixteen dollars? That isn't what I was told over the phone." A little old lady with curly gray hair and her wrinkled mouth twisted into a snarl was currently glaring at me like I had lit a bag of kittens on fire in front of her.

"Well then I can give a call to your insurance and have a representative discuss your exact coverage." I could feel a headache tight across my forehead, like this conversation was about to reach into my skull, pinching my brain.

"No!" Yet another patient thought it was okay to scream at me. "I need you to honor the price you told me over the phone."

"All I can do is give a call to your insurance." I wasn't even the one who spoke to her on the phone and told her however much she thought this appointment was going to cost.

The little old lady glared at me like I was personally out to get her. She didn't thank me when I got a hold of her insurance and fixed whatever financial miscommunication happened before I even started working at Miller Smile's Dentistry.

"Told you so," she snapped at me, giving me a death glare as if she was putting me in my place. As if I had a secret vendetta, with malicious plots to overcharge my poor and defenseless elderly patients.

Everyone was stressed out.

Everyone was anxious. About their teeth. About the crazy cost and weird insurance policies that made no logical sense.

And the common denominator?

Everyone was taking it out on me.

I gave Emma the excuse that I was going on my break and she shrugged disinterestedly in reply. After I'd scurried off to the break room, and finally had a moment of privacy, everything hit me.

I bit my lip. Trying to open my eyes wider, as if the extra air would be enough to force back the tears.

My eyes were getting blurry and stinging around the edges, but I wasn't going to give in. Why would I start crying? This is what I wanted… I chose this job over my scent matches.

Oh my God.

I chose this job over my scent matches… and I *hated* it.

What the hell was I doing? Was I really cowering in the back of a dental office like my life was ending?

No. Fuck this.

I scrolled through my contacts.

Obviously, I couldn't bother my moms right now. They were getting to the point in their pregnancies where they needed step by step instructions on how to get in and out of a car. But which of my dads was going to be the least dramatic about this?

My finger hovered over Daddy-Lo.

I scrubbed the tears off my face and forced myself to smile. Not because I was happy, obviously, but because it would change the way that my voice sounded. Maybe make me sound like I was happy, and wasn't asking to be rescued from abysmal failure.

He picked up after one ring.

"Chloe?"

"Daddy-Lo?" I couldn't help it, I sniffled a little bit hearing his caring voice. I couldn't help it, after the day I was having.

"What happened?" His voice dropped low and serious.

This morning, I'd taken the bus, and now I couldn't stomach the thought of sitting calmly around all of those people. Not after I'd fucked up this badly on day one of what was supposed to be the start of my grand new life.

I'd already calculated how much I'd have to put aside in savings for the next month before I'd be able to get a car on my own. All of those calculations were trashed now, along with my hopes for a quiet secretarial position.

"Can you pick me up?" I texted Daddy-Lo with the address to my job. Screw it.

All of my dads were over-protective, but I was past the point of caring.

"Be right there. Don't you worry about a thing, baby-girl."

His voice was clipped and all business. Nothing like his normal goofy dad-voice.

Well, shit.

A slight prickle of anxiety slithered up my spine, but I ignored it. Daddy-Lo was definitely over-reacting. Part of me felt like I should go wait outside, or at least give some sort of half-hearted attempt to warn my coworkers that an angry alpha might be bursting into this not-so-quiet dental office, but—meh.

If the Dentist and coworkers were so confident that they could treat someone like shit, just for being an omega... they could surely deal with the fallout.

This was on them.

CHAPTER 33
CHLOE

I WIPED my tears away and checked my makeup. My mascara was still doing its job. All I needed was to retouch my lipstick a tad. There.

It didn't even look at all like I had a complete emotional breakdown after realizing that all of my hopes and dreams for job fulfillment and prosperity had gone to live in the trash can.

Why hadn't anyone told me that working at a front desk was so soul sucking and miserable? It wasn't my oasis of quiet at all. Why did anyone choose to live like this?

Was it just this job, at this dental office? Or was it me? Was I cursed to live my life in hectic chaos?

Alright. Now I was spiraling. All I had to do was focus on keeping it together, just until my ride got here. Then I could make a hasty escape with Daddy-Lo and then none of these people would ever see me again.

I plastered my fake smile back on my face, and sat back down on my receptionist chair, waiting for the next tormentor to start giving me shit about insurance and co-payments and everything.

Suddenly, glass exploded across the lobby. Reflexively, I

swung my elbow up, guarding my face. It took me a second to register the heavily muscular man who rolled into a crouch, with an assault rifle slung across his shoulders—the man who'd leapt straight through the dental lobby windows —as Mag-Dad.

Oh shit.

If he was here… did that mean ALL my dads were showing up?

He had an expression of deadly calm as he scanned the perimeter, reaching around to grab his assault rifle.

Glass crunched behind him as a heavily tattooed man, with scars and burn marks littered across his face and biceps leapt through the window into the lobby, flanked by a white haired man with his blue eyes blazing, and throwing knives clenched in each hand: Pa Nix and Daddy Lo.

The door slammed open, the remaining glass panels shattered, as a giant stepped inside. Nearly seven feet tall and built like a mountain with an auburn beard that flowed down to his chest, Father was intimidating on the best of days. His presence made the entire lobby seem to shrink to half of its size.

Bringing up the rear, Daddy Gee had green and black camouflage paint smeared across his face as he strode in, sniper rifle in hand. Following close behind, Papa Diesel had a huge metal cylinder over his shoulder, with something that looked like a torpedo with an angry shark face painted over it.

"Chloe!" Father roared, as if I was a football field away and not in the same room as him separated by about a dozen feet. I battled the part of me that sort of wanted to hide under the counter and melt into the floor from embarrassment, but forced myself to stay where I was and give them a little half-hearted wave.

I thought that my dads might overreact, but even for them, this was a bit much.

"Is that a rocket launcher?" Oh my God, this was so fucking embarrassing. I tried to hide my face in my hands, when a strong grip uncovered my face. Father was looking me up and down, searching for any signs of injuries.

As my dads came closer to me, the patients in the lobby took the opportunity to back away and run out of the broken glass windows and escape to the parking lot.

The acid scent of urine flooded the air.

Emma was shaking and ducked under the counter as if this was an earthquake drill. I quickly averted my eyes from the sight of her wet pants.

Well, I'm not gonna lie, I was a little bit pissed at her for the snide hints that omegas couldn't handle office jobs, but that didn't mean that I wanted her to piss herself.

"What have they done to you?" Daddy Gee gently stroked my cheek. His gaze narrowed in on my eyes. I thought that I'd done a good enough job hiding the fact that I'd been crying, but the way that Daddy Gee was glaring daggers, that was not the case.

Ronald Brown ran out of his treatment room, with his mouth swollen and with the blue bib thing still clipped around his neck. He was wide-eyed, running like his life depended on it.

Ronald was still here? His appointment started hours ago, what did this dude do to his teeth? I just crossed my arms and watched him go.

Dr. Miller came charging out into the lobby not long after, still holding a dental probe. "What's going..."

The sentence died in his mouth at the sight of a full pack of heavily armed and enraged alphas.

Shit... he was holding something that looked like a weapon.

Well, it kind of looked like a weapon. If you squinted—it was metal and had a sharp pointy end... which was menacing enough for a pack of enraged men who were already on a warpath.

Father snarled, grabbing Dr. Miller by the throat and slamming him into the wall. He bent down to leer straight into his face.

"What. The. Fuck. Did you do to our daughter?" Father's face twisted into an angry snarl.

"D-daughter?" Dr. Miller's eyes went round, his jaw dropped. I could practically see the little hamster wheel spinning in his mind as he tried to process who the hell all these angry alphas were talking about. His darting gaze landed on me—given the fact that three of my dads were huddling around me and fussing like nervous mother hens, I guess he connected the dots to who their daughter was. "I didn't do anything to her, I swear!"

Father turned to me for confirmation.

"You are going to get me fired." I muttered.

It was really just to say something at this point, it wasn't like I wanted to work here anymore.

"Yeah, well, the men in this office should worry that we don't fire them." Papa Diesel aimed his rocket launcher at Dr. Miller who pressed himself harder against the wall.

I rolled my eyes, but inside the gesture loosened something inside of me that I didn't even realize was tight—until I was feeling weightless.

I stepped away from my post at the front desk, shaking my head. "I just said that I needed a ride. I didn't need all of this."

Daddy Gee and Mag-dad each slung an arm around my shoulders, shepherding me out of the lobby. Each of them turned to give death glares to Dr. Miller that he *possibly* didn't deserve—though angry enough that their glares made it clear that they would follow through in a heart-beat.

Daddy Gee leaned close to whisper into my ears, "Don't

worry about a thing pumpkin, we're going to take care of everything."

Father flung a business card on to the counter. "You can make a statement to our lawyers. Make sure to explain to them in detail *exactly* what you were doing with our daughter." Father's eyes narrowed, and a little vein was bulging right at his temple.

If Momma Rain was here, she would be pissed. Order him to sit down and waddle over to the kitchen to put on a cup of chamomile tea… but I digress.

Getting into the SUV, all my dads piled in all around me.

Maybe having the love and support of a pack of dads wasn't normal. Not for anyone outside of a pack anyway. But I had six pairs of eyes looking out for me.

If this wasn't normal then maybe I just didn't want or need to be normal anyway.

CHAPTER 34
CHLOE

AS SOON AS I got home, I grabbed my noise canceling headphones, a bowl of ice cream (pistachio flavored—for obvious reasons I wasn't in the mood for vanilla, chocolate or strawberry), a handful of brownies and a poptart for good measure.

In short, I had everything I needed for my well-deserved mental breakdown.

Instead of perfect solitude, however, a knock came at my bedroom door.

When I saw who opened it, I groaned internally.

Papa Diesel was like a wall of towering six-pack, with just about every spare inch of skin on his chest inked up. He had an intricate tattoo of a dragon bursting out of the waves, mouth wide open and fangs bared—like it was ready to charge off his skin and launch straight into battle.

Honestly, if I was in any kind of physical danger, I might have my fingers crossed that Papa Diesel was the first one to get there. I'm sure he could tear through my enemies like a bowling ball scatters pins.

If only my enemies were more interesting than an ornery

middle-aged dentist with more sarcasm than sense, then I might be in luck.

But I wasn't.

Papa Diesel had the dubious honor of being my biological father. Though his DNA wasn't a strike for or against him or anything.

In some packs, the kids were somewhat closer to their biological parent—which was kind of bullshit. They were *all* my dads. We were a family, and it didn't matter which one of my parent's blood flowed through my veins.

But out of all my dads, Papa Diesel was by far the worst at helping his kids handle their emotions.

Okay honestly, my bio dad sort of sucked at it.

It wasn't because he had the emotional range of a drowning slug. No. Papa Diesel felt emotions, same as everyone else. It was more because he was about as good at talking about his feelings as a canary was at bench pressing two hundred pounds.

"Hey Peanut," Papa Diesel, ruffled my hair with his big meaty hand. Like I was four.

"Hey Papa," I tried and failed to keep all the stress of the day out of my voice.

"Okay, what's wrong, Peanut." Papa Diesel frowned at me. "Is it about that dentist? Because that was just your first job. They're not all going to be like that. Don't blame yourself for working for an asshole."

Maybe it was because Papa Diesel was trying so hard. The fact that he was trying... even asking me how I was feeling right now was a big stretch for him.

Maybe it was just because I'd worked so hard for so many months... neglecting self care in pursuit of a dream that was now looking more like a dead end.

Maybe it was because I wanted my scent matches... but how could I go back to them now, after I'd fucked everything up?

…barely a week ago, I left them because I needed to go and find myself. How was I supposed to come running back now… when it turns out the self I was trying to find, ended up being shitty.

After I hurt them… the men that I loved… and for what?

All I know is this—everything unleashed in a flood.

My eyes went from moisture prickling at the corner to trickles pouring down that I couldn't stop. My nose was doing that thing where it was starting to feel drippy. I was in a desperate need of tissues before gross snot entered into the equation.

All I wanted was to feel like a hot mess—not look like one too.

But now it was too late, and I couldn't stop the tears. They seemed to be pouring down.

I tried to get my words out and explain everything to Papa Diesel, but I might have been hyperventilating a little.

"It-t's just… all that studying, and all those tests. It was so much… and for what? I don't know why I did that, and I'm fucking everything up. And now they're going to hate me, and I don't know what to do." Once I got the words out, I rubbed my forehead, as if that would help me hold in all of the emotions that were threatening to drown me.

Why did I do all that?

Why hadn't I just talked to them about working? Instead of pushing them away…

How did I manage to fuck up my entire life, within a week of graduating from the Institute?

Had I really turned my back on the men I loved… in order to work for a minimum wage job?

By now, I was practically sobbing. It was bad. Like I was using the top of my shirt as a make-shift tissue. I'd probably have to throw the whole thing out by the time I got my emotions under control.

Papa Diesel was holding up his hands, like dealing with

his emotional omega daughter was somehow worse than a terrorist extremist negotiation.

"It's okay, Peanut." He was backing away, even as he attempted to reassure me. "How about I go get your Mother?"

Soft hands started rubbing my back. Hands that I knew.

"Hey Chloe-cutie," Mother crooned in her soft voice.

I wanted to hug her and bury my face in her warmth and let all of this mess disappear—except that she was like a thousand months pregnant and I didn't want to like, give her affection that was too aggressive and trigger early labor or something.

I sniffed loudly and rubbed some of the tears out of my eyes to get a good look at her instead. Mother sat by my side and Daddy-Gee was next to her, providing support. Perhaps more than just emotional support. It looked like he was holding her arm so that she wouldn't go toppling over. I guess balancing gets trickier when one knows that they have feet, but can't see them. Or maybe Mother had one of the dads by her side in case her fetus decided it wanted to pop out early.

"What's going on, my Chloe-cutie-pie?" Mother looked tired. She was always tired this late into pregnancy. But her concern was still warm and comforting.

If anyone could help me sort out this mess that I'd gotten myself into, it was Mother. No matter how exhausted she was from growing yet another sibling, Mother would give me good advice.

I'd worked my ass off for the entire Institute program, and finished my online Associates degree a year early. Why the fuck did I feel such a burning need to do all that?

I don't know who I was trying to prove myself to—it

didn't seem like anyone cared how academically accomplished I was. All I'd managed to do was to stress myself out.

I'd thought that working at my dream job would make it all worth it. I had even filled one notebook with detailed plans for what I was going to do with the money… Maybe in a couple of years I'd even be able to afford to go on a vacation to some vacant island in the middle of nowhere.

But obviously, all of those plans had gone to shit. All that remained of all that effort were the stains left behind on the bottom of the toilet bowl after my dreams had been flushed away.

"Why did no one ever tell me that a secretary job would be so awful?" I crossed my arms around my chest, my gaze fixed on the unfinished bowl of ice cream on my desk that was slowly melting into a sad puddle.

Daddy-Gee looked like he was struggling not to laugh, hiding his laugh behind a coughing fit.

"Oh, Sweetheart," Mother cooed, elbowing Daddy-Gee sharply in the side. He yelped and got himself together. "Were you expecting the job to be a bit more exciting?"

"Well, no," I admitted.

Okay. So honestly, I took this job because I was sick of all the excitement and was ready for something stable and boring.

I just wasn't expecting the quiet and boring job to be so… well, *boring*.

Well, I would have been fine if *boring* was the only problem. When that job wasn't boring, it was psychologically damaging. Why did people think it was okay to take all of their aggression out on receptionists?

Their poor planning and lack of communication skills were *not* my fault.

"Ugh, I can't believe that I gave up my scent matches to work at a dental office," I ran both my fingers through my hair, mussing it up.

"Wait, what? Since when has my Baby got scent matches?" Daddy-Gee was looking at the door, like he was just about ready to go track down my alphas and beat them up just for existing.

Mother silenced him with a sharp, "Genesis!"

"Sorry, Honey," Daddy-Gee muttered.

"Can you tell us what happened?" Mother soothed a palm down my forehead, smoothing down my hair.

"I thought that all I wanted was a bit of peace and quiet. This job was supposed to be that. It was going to be the start of a brand-new life. I was going to prove myself. But it wasn't quiet, it was filled with assholes, and I hated every minute of it."

Mother nodded encouragingly, showing me that she was listening.

"And it's one thing that I have to give up on my career dreams. Just like last week, I practically broke up with my scent matches so that I could start working there." I'd given up everything... any chance for a social life back at the Institute. Vast chunks of my mental health. Worst of all, I'd hurt my alphas... so that I could fetch coffee for asshole dentists.

"Chloe... just because they're your scent matches doesn't mean that you need to feel forced to be with them."

Mother probably thought that I was using the work thing as an excuse not to bond them... which couldn't be further from the truth.

I shook my head. "It's not like that. I love them."

"Well then, is there any reason why you can't go be with your alphas?" Mother was tilting her head to the side as she pursed her lips. It was as if she could see the dots in this conversation and had no idea how they connected.

Ha.

So that was a great question Mother brought up. Why couldn't I just be with my alphas?

Even though it was hard to admit it, even to myself... the

answer was yes. Though I'd tried to pretend like everything was fine… I *did* have genuine concerns about being with my scent matches.

I took a deep breath, bracing myself to be vulnerable. This was a safe space. Who was better than Mother to help me sort through my deepest and darkest fears?

"You know how my scent is vanilla? They are chocolate, strawberry and banana. Together we literally smell like a neapolitan banana split."

Mother pinched her lips together, forcing herself not to react.

Daddy-Gee didn't have that kind of restraint.

"That sounds really serious… " then he dropped the sarcastic tone and whatever else he was going to say as Mother glared at him.

Okay, my parents weren't acting like the scent thing was a big deal… Maybe I was overreacting about that…

But that wasn't even the biggest issue.

"That's not even the worst part. Their last name is Fanny. If I accepted them… we would all be known as the Fanny Pack." Tears started to well up, stinging my eyes again… even after I thought I'd cried them all out. "I'm going to be known as the omega from the Fanny Pack."

Mother winced each time I said their pack name. So, I knew that things weren't looking good. But I really knew that I was right to be concerned about the last name when Daddy-Gee didn't even crack a dumb joke about it.

"You know, it's alright for the pack to choose the name of one of the other alphas, if they all agreed on it. It doesn't need to be based on the Pack lead." Daddy-Gee's voice was grim, any hint of laughter completely gone.

"They already offered me that." I shook my head. If the solution was that simple, I wouldn't be sitting on my bed, bawling my eyes out.

I probably wouldn't have been so quick to tell Kain that I

needed space.

In all honesty, if things were just a little different, I probably would have agreed to move in with them, like I wanted to.

"Besides the Fanny twins there's one other alpha I'm scent matched to. His name is…" I wiped the rest of the tears away. I just had to say it. "His name is Brutus Back. I'm not going to ask them to change their name just to become… the Back Pack."

I didn't even know that there was a pack name that was worse than the Fanny pack. Couldn't even have imagined it until I heard Brutus' last name.

How the fuck did I end up with an alternative name that was even worse, when I'd started with the Fanny pack?

"Chloe, I'm not going to lie… neither of those choices are ideal." Mother took my hand in hers, squeezing it in reassurance. "But I also know this. I didn't raise my daughter to be a quitter. You told me that you love them. Do you really want to give up your alphas because they have silly last names?"

I squeezed Mother's hand back.

Mother was right.

Did I want to be known as Chloe, former member of the Stryker pack, former omega Valedictorian… now a part of the Fanny pack? Or even worse, the Back pack?

Obviously not.

But did I want to leave them over it?

No.

I couldn't. Even now. I missed them.

If I was being completely honest with myself, all I really wanted to do was to reach out to them. Find them. Apologize to them until I'd fixed what I'd broken between us.

As soon as she asked me the question, I knew in my heart what I had to do.

If they even wanted to see my sorry ass after I'd gone and broken their hearts just last week.

CHAPTER 35

CHLOE

OKAY, two things were clear.

I'd been an idiot and needed to apologize to my alphas immediately.

And I had no idea how to go about doing it.

What the fuck was I going to say to them? Were they even going to want to talk to me after the confusing bullshit I'd pulled?

Ughh.

I fell face first on my bed, refusing to let my thoughts spiral into doom anymore. If I did that, I would start crying again, and I had only just gotten my face back to normal.

Plus, my eyes would be stinging… again.

No. I wasn't going to sit there and obsess over the best way of reaching out to them, or draft out the perfect text message to send to them. I'd just see if they wanted to meet me in person.

Me: Hey

Immediately, three bubbles popped up… and went away.

After a moment, the three bubbles popped up again. Only to vanish into the communication text void once more.

When the anticipation was really threatening to kill me, I decided, fuck it. I wasn't about to wait to see the carefully articulated message Kain was constructing.

Me: Can I come over?

This time his response was immediate.

Kain: Yes

Once again, I found myself standing in front of the Fanny pack house, filled with apprehension. Though this time it was somehow worse... before I'd been vaguely worried that I was about to meet an alpha who had to be hidden away in an attic somewhere to stop him from murderous rampages or something.

Now I was just worried that I'd gone and made the stupidest mistake in my life. Perhaps one that was unfixable, and that I would spend the rest of my miserable life alone... maybe working at a different dental office... never to find love again.

Great, now I was spiraling, again.

No, it was fine. Today I had a plan, and I hadn't come empty handed.

I rang their doorbell, giving myself a mental pep talk and reminder that I could do this, and almost immediately the door was yanked open.

All three of my alphas stood in the doorway, crowding the space. My handsome, very built, very *tense* men.

"Hi," I said, holding the three bouquets in front of me like a shield. I'd made a pit stop in the middle of ride-sharing, stopping at the grocery store next to Brutus' favorite salon, and ran in to buy them.

"Did... someone get you flowers?" Kain frowned at the bouquets.

Well, it had seemed like a good idea, in the middle of panicking on the drive over.

"No. I was an asshole. I needed to make it up to you somehow." I handed a bouquet to each of my alphas. Sabien got the marigold and daisy one in bright yellow and oranges that reminded me of his fiery side. Sabien tilted his head at the bouquet, like he'd never seen a flower before and didn't know what to do with it. I can't read minds, but he looked like he was thinking, what do I do with this, eat it? For Kain I'd gotten bright pink peonies and hydrangeas in soft pinks and blues because they had looked romantic and lovely.

As I handed Brutus his dozen white roses, he grasped my hand along with the bouquet, brushing his thumb along my inner wrist... causing warmth to bloom all the way across my body. Then Brutus took the flowers and nodded like they were his due. He stepped into the house, rummaging around the kitchen cabinets before pulling out a crystal vase. After filling it with water, he deposited them, taking a moment to arrange them.

"You didn't need to get me flowers," Kain shook his head, stepping into the house and waving me in.

"But I did though." I was wringing my hands now.

Was I defending the need to buy flowers in the first place? Well, Brutus clearly liked them, so it worked for one out of three. I don't know, maybe chocolates would have been better for the twins... but I hadn't known what to do. All I knew was that I couldn't come here empty handed.

Kain's gaze was fixed on the flowers in his hands, the cellophane crinkling in his grip as he placed his bouquet down gently on the coffee table. "Does this mean that you're coming back to us?"

"Uhh… yeah." My voice went up high like I was asking a question, but I definitely didn't mean it as a question. It's just that I practiced a whole speech in the car ride over, and hadn't even gotten a chance to deliver it—you know, how this was all a mistake. That I never should have left them in the first place… how I loved them.

Yeah, I never even told them that. I should probably get around to—

All of a sudden, strong arms wrapped around me, as I was tipped back and literally swept off my feet. Then Kain's warm lips were on mine, kissing me hungrily.

I closed my eyes, lost in the kiss. In the heat and the delicious friction, in the sweep of his tongue as he deepened the kiss. In the way that he made me feel like I was coming alive. Like every single inch of my body was a stringed instrument, vibrating with tension and he was the musician ready to rock my world.

"I missed you." Kain brushed his finger along my cheek, tracing the curve of my jaw. "I've been wanting to do that since the moment you left."

I nodded breathless.

"Was there something else that was bothering you?" Kain let me put my feet back on the ground, but didn't let me go. Those strong arms were still wrapped around me, keeping me safe as Kain dug deeper, asking me to reveal why—the real reason why I'd left in the first place.

I hesitated. My issues with their last name were my own problem and I would just deal with it. But bringing it up in front of my alphas was a whole nother story. It wasn't fair to them, it was an integral part of them, and something that they had no control over.

Like what if they told me that they hated my hair color? How would I face that hatred towards something I was born with… besides maybe the need to buy some dye or something.

"It wasn't anything you did…" I had to say it. From now on, I was going to commit myself to honesty and transparency. "I have to admit that I was a little freaked out when I learned your last name."

"That's fair," Sabien shrugged. "Our last name is pretty freaking weird."

I swallowed down the lump that had formed in my throat. Well… Sabien had taken that well. *Extremely* well.

Is that all I needed to do? If I had just had a short conversation about my feelings with the guys, would that have been enough to stop all this unnecessary drama that had sprouted between us?

"I promise," Kain's brilliant blue eyes filled with fiery determination. "If what you need is for none of us to ever wear a fanny pack again. That is what we will do. No one in this pack will ever even *think* of touching a fanny pack if it bothers you."

I sniffed. Determined not to start crying again… unless they were happy tears. Those were okay, I guess.

What was finding love compared to having to deal with having a stupid name? Obviously, love should win out.

"Anything my darling girl needs." Kain continued, grasping my hands and squeezing reassuringly. "Well, we don't have to exactly follow tradition. We can take on Brutus' name if that makes you more comfortable."

"No." I said too quickly. "I mean, you don't have to do that."

Really.

Don't do that.

I was rubbing my forehead… this meeting wasn't going at all how I pictured it. Everything that I thought was going to happen was going wrong. Not all of them liked the flowers…

they hadn't even listened to my speech. Did it make sense to even recite the whole thing now?

"I just want you to know that I'm sorry for hurting you." It wasn't anything close to my full speech. Even that hadn't felt like enough. Originally, I was going to make a PowerPoint presentation with a multi-step apology plan… but ultimately I managed to get to the heart of what I'd wanted to say (though obviously it would be more thorough with the power point. I'd even picked out the color scheme and everything).

"There's nothing to forgive." Kain shook his head. "You needed to be sure, and there's nothing wrong with that."

Well, Kain was sweet, though a bit misguided. I *had* put them through unnecessary pain. But if he was going to forgive me, I wasn't about to complain.

I brushed my fingertips along his cheeks, just above his rugged jawline, as I looked into the depths of his ocean eyes. "I love you."

A grin spread across Kain's handsome features. He leaned his forehead against mine, shutting his eyes like he was basking in my presence. "I love you too."

I felt floaty and giddy, like I'd turned into a bottle of soda that had gotten tossed around, and if anyone opened me up right now, I would explode. This was everything I'd ever wanted and—

Our romantic moment was interrupted, as Sabien approached, eyes on me and completely ignoring his brother as he pulled me into his arms.

Well that was kind of rude, could he not read the room?

Or was this jealousy since I'd admitted my feelings for his brother? I mean I loved them all… but he needed to give me a minute. If I went up to each of my alphas one by one to say the words, that felt like it cheapened the moment.

"Well, if you still want to make things up to us," there was no mistaking the hunger in Sabien's eyes, "I can think of something."

"Absolutely the fuck not." Brutus rose out of his leather chair, walking toward Sabien like a predator. He towered over Sabien, grabbing his chin and forcing him to meet the burning heat in his dark eyes. "I've let you get away with too much. That ends now." Brutus was looking at Sabien like he was a cut of prime rib and he was dying to get a taste. "You, me and our Baby girl. In my room."

CHAPTER 36
CHLOE

SO THAT'S how I found myself once again, legs spread on Brutus' pristine black sheets.

Sabien was in between my thighs, rubbing circles around my clit that were slowly and steadily pushing me to the edge. I was almost seeing stars, panting and out of control, when Sabien stopped. All of a sudden he was groaning, and barely able to hold himself up on the bed.

Brutus grabbed Sabien by the neck and brought him face to face with the anger etched on to his features. "Did I tell you that you could stop pleasuring our omega?"

"No." Sabien was breathless, sounding nothing like the confident alpha I knew. It seemed like everyone melted into butter when faced with the Brutus' primal dominance.

Brutus pulled Sabien closer, kissing him passionately in a heated kiss, grabbing his ass hard enough to bruise. It was possessive and wild, and I felt myself getting wetter as Brutus started stroking and teasing Sabien's hole.

Brutus broke off the kiss, maneuvering Sabien back on top of me. "Then pleasure her," he growled in his deep voice that had Sabien shuddering.

Then Sabien brought his lips down to mine, kissing me

hard. He took my mouth deeply, as he pressed his strong body against mine, touching every part of me. He cupped my breasts, pinching lightly at my nipples until I was losing my mind.

I called out his name, desperate. Writhing beneath him, as his hands once again began to tease my entrance. Starting a rhythm that was making me lose sense of everything but the friction, the pressure right there where I needed it. He circled my clit until I whimpered, grasping the sheets in a white-knuckled grip… just needing something to hold on to. Because the way that the pressure was building in my core was threatening to make me lose every shred of myself.

The tension was coiling and tightening within me, and then his fingers slid against my clit just right, and everything unleashed in a pulsing wave. Pleasure erupted out of my core, white hot and intense. Thrumming across my body, like a bolt of electric heat, lighting up my spine and all the way down to my fingertips and toes.

I panted heavily. My body went all limp on the bed as I caught my breath. Sabien was pressing light kisses along my neck as I recovered from how hard I came. Distantly, I heard the light pad of footsteps, and then water running, as Brutus washed his hands in his en-suite bathroom.

The bed creaked as Brutus rejoined us, with a bottle of lube in hand. Brutus wrapped his hand around Sabien's neck possessively, squeezing lightly. Pulling Sabien closer to whisper something into his ear.

I didn't have the energy to lift myself off the mattress to try to hear what they were talking about, but Brutus' tone was low and threatening and I saw Sabien's dick twitch in response.

Brutus dropped fat globs of lube in his hands, which he used to coat the full length of his magnificent dick. Then he squeezed lube right onto Sabien's ass, massaging it in deep with his finger.

Brutus leaned close to Sabien's ear, close enough for me to hear him say, "you better fuck her good," before slapping Sabien's ass hard.

Sabien's breath hitched, before his gaze locked on me. Blue eyes blown wide with lust. All of his wild energy, laser focused right on me.

I licked my lips in anticipation, spreading my legs wider for him.

Sabien wasted no time, before he thrust into me deep, filling me completely.

I moaned—so stuffed with his big cock.

Feeling him against my walls, the rough stretch... the intense friction all at once. It was fucking exquisite.

Then Sabien began to really move, pounding into me like a man possessed. He took me—hard. Our hips crashed together, again and again. His heavy balls were slapping into my ass.

With one brutal stroke, Brutus slammed into Sabien, bottoming out, pushing Sabien even deeper inside of me— fucking into both of us.

Sabien groaned, a masculine sound laced with pleasure.

"You're mine," Brutus growled. He was rocking into Sabien, dominating the rhythm with each thrust, until he was fucking us both.

As if he was fucking me through Sabien.

"And any alpha belonging to me will know the meaning of a good fuck." Brutus grabbed Sabien's hip in a bruising grip, diving into him with savage thrusts—each one had Sabien slamming deep into me, his hips grinding against mine. Right against my clit.

The friction was so intense, it was threatening to knock me over. Rip me up and shred me to pieces. Reforming me into an omega who knew, without question, that this was right where I belonged. Right where I wanted to be—with my alpha's cock moving furiously inside me.

"Don't you dare slow down. You want this knot, you better earn this knot." Brutus said through gritted teeth.

With a strangled moan, Sabien picked up the pace, until he was rutting into me like a madman, chasing after pleasure. Thrusting into me over and over as the base of his cock thickened.

Sabien grunted helplessly, and then he was cumming hard. Jets of his cum flooded me as his knot popped, locking him inside me.

With a roar, Brutus thrust in deep as he came, knotting Sabien.

"Take it. That's it." Brutus murmured into Sabien's ear, "you're mine."

Brutus wrapped his arms around both of us, pulling carefully until we were all lying sideways in the bed, like an assortment of spoons two big and one little.

Panting and locked together in the aftermath of explosive pleasure.

All in all, I'd say that my apology was a success.

To think that I was afraid of exactly this—of spending my days surrounded by alphas who cared about me. Who pleasured me.

These men, they were mine. Now that I had gotten that drilled into my thick skull, I wasn't going to give them up for anything…

(but especially not for any office receptionist job).

CHAPTER 37
CHLOE

SABIEN AND KAIN trudged through the door, dragging their feet like they had just labored a few days under the hot sun, while getting continuously bitten by rabid chihuahuas.

Which they hadn't—they'd just gone to an interview with my dads.

Brutus was the only one of my alphas who looked composed. He casually opened the fridge, grabbing the pitcher he kept inside, and poured himself a glass of water. I mean, it was Brutus. I would have been shocked if he wasn't composed.

"So… how did it go?" I sat on the soft black leather couch, in between the twins, looking from Kain's drained face to Sabien's blank expression (it must have been a bit much for him if he was dissociating this hard, poor guy).

Father had already texted me, saying that it went great.

He and the rest of my dads probably loved the idea of getting to grill their daughter's scent matches.

For the love of God, they better not make this into a new family tradition. Cashmere was still looking for her alphas. Also, my younger sisters were all rather young. What if they ended up being omegas? If they found out that our dads were going to grill their alphas all because they were worried about my *tiny* little mental breakdown after quitting Miller Smile's, my sisters would kill me.

It wasn't quite fair… though I guess I sort of expected it. What was more shocking was they hadn't thought to interview any of Rebel's alphas.

At least they weren't being sexist… strictly speaking. Since I had interviewed pretty much every single alpha who was a finalist for Titus' pack (which I think meant, that he sent all the hottest guys to get interviewed by me).

"Honestly, that was fucking terrifying." Sabien admitted outright.

"Well, yeah." I shrugged. "My dads can be a bit…*much* sometimes."

"Wasn't just your dads. A bunch of your brothers were there too."

"What!?" *Assholes.*

Why did my brothers think they had the right to go stick their nose in my business? I mean, true I'd done that for all of the alphas who'd wanted to get into Titus's pants, but he *asked* me for help. More like manipulated me into helping, with the threat of him living a life of regret and heartbreak with his poor choices.

"Yeah, I've never been interviewed by a panel of eleven men before." Kain was wiping imaginary sweat off his brows.

Eleven?

What the fuck were my brothers playing at? That was every single one of my brothers (at least the ones who had grown out of diapers,) interviewing my scent matches.

You know what, actually it was fine. None of my brothers had chosen omegas yet for their packs… It was only *fair* that I now get a chance to return the favor.

"Okay then, there's only one thing left to do."

Kain sighed heavily. Then nodded, like he was expecting

me to come up with a part two to this stupid interview process to find his pack worthy.

I smiled coyly. "Now you just need to bite me."

It was like my words dumped cold water on every man in the room, shocking them into action. Brutus rushed over from the kitchen, his second glass of water still in hand. Sabien stared at me slack jawed.

"Wait, what? Already?" Kain yelped.

"Yeah, why not." I shrugged. I knew what I wanted. I knew that my alphas were *it* for me. So what was the point of waiting any longer?

"Do people throw a celebration for this sort of thing?" Sabien glanced at his packmates frantically.

"We should go get a cake or something." Kain looked over at the key rings, where his car fob dangled as if he was planning on running out the door now.

"You can bite me like that shoe commercial—just do it." I smiled.

Kain took in a deep breath and cracked his neck. "Are you sure you want this? You want to bond us?" He asked me in a quiet voice.

I nodded. Yeah, I was sure. Ever since regret smacked me full across the face at the Smile's dental clinic.

"If that's what you want," Kain murmured.

He placed a sweet kiss on my lips, then trailed hot kisses down my neck.

I felt a sharp edge of teeth, and then a pinch. If I had to admit it, I was expecting it to hurt, but it was Kain's mouth against my neck. More than bracing for pain, I felt a fluttery feeling in my stomach, and the rapid beating of my heart.

Then Kain bit down, breaking through my skin.

There was a brief slice of pain… then a shimmery explosion that ripped across my mind. Blowing my thoughts away… as it opened my mind to them.

I could feel them… my head was full of emotions that

weren't mine. But at the same time, I *knew* them. I knew these men like I knew myself. Like I knew my own heart.

I sat for a moment, sorting through the emotions. Sabien's brewing storm of wild energy… Kain's fierce determination. There was even Brutus' quiet confidence… and joy.

As the thoughts settled, I focused on the energy of the bond—it felt like floating. Like being spun around in the arms of a lover. Cool and brilliant, rising to the top of my brow like a regal caress.

"You offered me the princess bond?" I gasped.

"Well yeah." Kain scratched the back of his head.

"But doesn't that mean that you guys won't be able to get another omega?"

Brutus placed his glass of water down abruptly on the coffee table, shaking his head like the very idea of another omega was ridiculous. "Why would we want another omega when we have you?"

CHAPTER 38
BRUTUS

I'D FINALLY GOTTEN Chloe away for a trip to Nesting Needs.

I couldn't wait to help Chloe build the nest of her dreams.

"Go, crazy Love. We can get anything your heart desires."

Chloe smiled widely as she power walked down the first aisle.

The first item that she threw into the shopping cart was a small pack of fairy lights.

Alright. People needed staples. Maybe she wasn't sure exactly what she wanted and needed to get some lights to test the waters.

There wasn't anything wrong with liking fairy lights.

Chloe took a leisurely stroll down the aisles, passing by some mood lighting fixtures with great architectural details. She stopped once she got to the Himalayan salt lamp, read the description on the back before placing it next to the fairy lights.

Okay. If my Baby girl wanted the generic salt lamp, my girl got that.

"Oh, I like this," Chloe exclaimed as she picked up a pink neon sign that said breathe.

I chuckled, amused at her little joke… until she placed it in the shopping cart with the rest of the things.

Ah. She actually wasn't joking.

Alright then, that was my mistake.

She then went on and completely bypassed the entire aisle that had high-end metallic accessories, as well as various types of vases.

God, we needed to go back to that aisle at some point. Chloe needed a minimum of two crystal vases. How was I even supposed to get my girl any flowers without that? At this point, it wasn't even something I wanted, it was a room essential.

Then, Chloe started heading toward a section of rugs. The textures in fabrics had the potential to make drastic changes in the feel of a room. She could easily turn her nest space into something that felt sultry and sophisticated… especially with a vibrant piece like that Turkish cotton. Or Chloe couldn't go wrong with that modern Persian or even the hand-woven Moroccan tassel… but no, Chloe walked past all of those to grab a lavender dyed shag carpet… made from synthetic fibers.

Everything that she was touching was so… basic.

Which was fine.

I just had to remind myself that this was Chloe's space. She was picking the exact items in her nest that would help her feel safe. There wasn't any rule anywhere that said that the items that made her feel most comfortable had to be high-end or luxurious in any way.

Well, however my omega chose to decorate her room, there was no way that she could end up making it look worse than Sabien's pig sty. If worse came to worst, I would just pretend that the nest didn't exist. We could always fuck in different rooms of the house.

I generally made it a rule with my lovers not to interfere with their preferences. I strove to make them happy… but

Chloe had just thrown sheets into the shopping bin without even looking at the thread count. When I grabbed the package and checked it, they were really at a thread count of one-hundred forty-four.

Absolutely not.

I drew the line at safety. This thread count was so low, it was going to give us all breakouts and eczema when Chloe's heat hit. I refused to fuck on sheets that were this cheap—at that point we might as well just be rolling around on the mud, or in the literal hay. This was disgusting.

I cleared my throat to get her attention. I would be gentle about this and bring it up in a way that wouldn't violate her autonomy. "Are you sure you don't want this in Egyptian cotton?"

"Oh. What's that?" Chloe had a breezy voice. She wasn't even looking at the sheets anymore, she was checking out an oversized dream catcher. I didn't even need to get closer to read the label jutting from the side that said it was made in China.

Holy shit.

My girl… didn't know what Egyptian cotton was?

I forced myself to control the expression on my face. I wasn't going to look shocked. I wasn't going to express any horror. I refused to make a scene in a nesting store and make a huge deal over linen thread counts. "It's made with higher quality material, so it's softer and more durable."

"I guess that sounds nice. But do you know where—"

I grabbed the sheets that I'd been eyeing, hoping that Chloe would choose. They were the same color she'd chosen but with a thread count of eight hundred; it was a much healthier choice for our skin. Not enough people realized how much bacteria could grow in low-quality linen.

While I was off grabbing the proper bed sheets, Chloe grabbed a throw pillow with the words "live, laugh, love" stitched on. My eye twitched involuntarily at the sight of it—

but it was fine. As long as the pillow was meant to be decorative, and no human head actually had to come in contact with it, the cheap fabric wouldn't harm anybody. Most likely.

The next box that Chloe chucked into the shopping cart was for an incense kit—one where the ceramic holder was shaped like a Buddha. My mind raced to think of excuses to get out of this aisle before—

"Oh! These are so pretty!" Chloe was hunched over a display of crystals. "Should I get a rose quartz or amethyst?"

I placed my hand over my mouth like I was lost in thought, as I attempted to hold back from voicing an opinion about her chosen design aesthetic.

Okay. So my omega was a bit of a *basic bitch*.

Okay fine. That was fine.

As long as she kept buying the good sheets for me to fuck her on... did it really matter?

ABOUT THE AUTHOR

I'm Miyo Hunter and I'm addicted to Dominant Alphas. Sweet love and dark fantasy. From shifters to omegaverse, I want characters bent over chairs and called a good girl. I want to read until jobs and responsibilities don't exist. Until I'm lost in a world that's spicy and a little bit wild.

If you enjoyed reading, please leave a review. Honest reviews help other readers find books they may enjoy.

instagram.com/miyohunter
tiktok.com/@miyohunter

ALSO BY MIYO HUNTER

Moonlight Reborn

He was the most dominant wolf in the pack and I'm the bullied outcast he hates until his skin touched mine, electricity sparked. Marking us. We both knew what it meant—a soulbond.

Moonlight Shifter

Finding your soulmate is every wolf shifter's dream—except mine. I'm already in love. So when destiny revealed my mate, I did the only thing I could. I ran from him. But no matter how strong I am, a lone wolf is vulnerable. When I'm captured, the only one who can come for me, is the mate I'd rejected.

His Gold Pack Omega

A shattered omega socialite, rejected by society.

After what I went through, becoming an outcast was the only way to survive. But now none of the laws protecting omegas apply to me.

I hired him to be my bodyguard. He's all raw strength, gorgeous and protective.I feel drawn to him, and the heat in his gaze makes me feel alive again. For the first time in years, I feel safe. But how can I let him in without letting him see the broken thing I've become?

Moonlight Claimed—coming soon!

We hid our identities at the Shifter's Masked Ball, but I still managed to find my soulmate among the sea of masked faces and smothered scents.

While I thought he was everything I'd ever wanted, I realized several sweaty and delicious minutes later that I'd made a horrible mistake.

Is it too late to reject him now that my fate is sealed? Or could this unlikely bond be exactly what I've been waiting for?

THE POISONVERSE

Havoc Killed Her Alpha - *Marie Mackay*
Forget Me Knot - *Marie Mackay*
Pack of Lies - *Olivia Lewin*
Ruined Alphas - *Amy Nova*
Sweetheart - *Marie Mackay*
Lonely Alpha - *Olivia Lewin*
And more to come…

Shorts:
His Gold Pack Omega - *Miyo Hunter*
Something Knotty Something Blue - *Lilith K.Duat*